Christmas at the Hummingbird House

Center Point
Large Print

Also by Donna Ball and available from
Center Point Large Print:

A Wedding on Ladybug Farm
The Hummingbird House

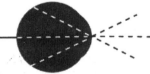

**This Large Print Book carries the
Seal of Approval of N.A.V.H.**

Christmas at the Hummingbird House

Donna Ball

CENTER POINT LARGE PRINT
THORNDIKE, MAINE

Christmas at the Hummingbird House

ONE

Ghosts of Christmas Past

Chicago, 1965

Andrew Norton was one of those people who liked to wait until the last minute to do his Christmas shopping. He insisted that it wasn't Christmas until you'd been caught in the mad gaiety of Marshall Fields half an hour before closing on Christmas Eve, been pushed along by the tidal wave of other last minute shoppers on Michigan Avenue, had dashed into shops ten minutes before closing or reached the checkout line at the mall just as the lights were flickering off. His wife had despaired of ever changing his habits, despite the fact that his Christmas Eve shopping adventures met with inconsistent success. A lighted umbrella from the hardware store had been the best he could do for his mother-in-law one memorable Christmas, and the battery-operated pineapple peeler he'd gotten from a street vendor for his sister was still talked about over holiday dinners twelve years later. In good years, however, his last-minute impulses yielded treasures that were as memorable as his failures: cashmere scarves at seventy percent off, a cameo

7

broach that had unexpectedly been spotted in an antique store window, silk pajamas, sapphire earrings, even a set of Craftsman tools for his do-it-yourself dad, half off at Sears at 11:45 p.m. on Christmas Eve.

This was a good year, mostly because it was the first time his daughter, now age seven, had been old enough to go with him. And because, while they both agreed that seven was an age of great distinction, she still had to be in bed by nine o'clock, the shopping wasn't quite as last-minute as it had been on previous occasions, and most of the better stores were still open. They had a magical visit with Santa followed by hot chocolate topped with melting marshmallows, and there was still time to join the crush at Marshall Fields where Angela chose a plush toy for her baby cousin and a jar of bath salts topped with a pink bow for her mother. They went back out into the blur of colored lights and bustling people, delighting in pointing out window displays and catching snowflakes on their tongues for a block or two. Andrew ducked into a crowded bookstore where he found a book on container gardening with gorgeous glossy photos for his mother-in-law, who liked that kind of thing, and a book on the history of aviation for his father-in-law, a retired airline pilot. He was on a roll.

They crossed the park at Water Tower Street, where the snow-covered trees were all decorated with twinkling white lights and carolers were singing "Silver Bells" on the corner. The air was crisp and cold with just enough snow to tickle the cheeks, and it smelled like the steamy hot dogs from the cart just ahead. It was close to eight o'clock and Andrew had promised his wife to have Angela home before bedtime, but he was half inclined to join the line that had formed in front of that hot dog cart. He knew, because he had so many wonderful memories of growing up himself, the value of moments like this. Angela skipped along beside him in her blue coat and matching hat, her mittened hand tucked securely into his, her cheeks apple-red with excitement and cold.

"Daddy," she said, eyes dancing and breath steaming as she looked up at him. "This is the best Christmas Eve ever! Can we go for a horse ride?"

He laughed and decided that bedtime came every night, but the best Christmas Eve ever came only once. "You bet, sweetheart." He changed direction toward the north corner, where they could cross the street and head toward the horse-drawn carriage stand. He hesitated when a block of golden light coming from a narrow street that ran beside the park caught his eye. He had never explored that particular street before, and though most of the few shops that lined it were already closed, the one from which the light spilled had a charming, Dickensian look and an even more inviting name. *Keepsakes and Treasures* was

9

written above the door in a Victorian font, and the display window was filled with the kind of tchotchkes and collectibles his wife adored.

He said, "Angel, honey, what do you say we stop in there and see if we can find a present for Mommy?" He pointed. "Horse ride right after, I promise."

She agreed cheerfully, "Okay, Daddy. Make sure they put a pink bow on it. Mommy loves pink."

An old-fashioned bell clattered over the door when they entered, and a man in a red plaid shirt smiled at them across the counter. A kind of cottony stillness descended when the door closed behind them, sealing out the clatter of the outside world and enfolding them in a cozy warmth that smelled of apple cider and fine old things.

"Merry Christmas, sir, young lady," the man greeted them. "What can I help you find this good evening?"

Andrew said, "I'm looking for something for my wife."

Angela wandered away as the two adults talked, exploring the treasures with eyes that darted from one lovely object to the next. The little shop was Aladdin's cave for a child, shelves and cabinets crowded with shiny things and pretty things: pictures in silver frames, tiny clocks, glass bottles, polished stones. She heard her daddy say, "Be careful, honey. Don't break anything."

She called back, "Okay, I won't." But even as

she said it she was reaching for a snow globe on the shelf in front of her.

The two men started talking again, and she heard the cash register ring as she held the glass globe in both of her plump hands. She turned it upside down and watched the snow swirl around a log house in the mountains. Her lips curved upward in a smile of delight as the snow cleared and settled on the roof, revealing a long porch with doors painted in happy colors, and light spilling out of the windows. There were Christmas wreaths on the doors, and she could see a Christmas tree inside one of the windows. Her smile widened as she wiped a smudge off the globe and found that she could actually see through the window and into the room. She brought the globe closer, squinting to see more.

There were people inside the room. There was a tall man with silver hair and another man wearing a purple jacket. They were smiling and talking. The tall man was standing in front of a Christmas tree that was decorated with silver and blue bows and covered with hundreds of tiny glass birds. There was a fire in the fireplace and the mantelpiece above it was all decorated with gold and silver branches. A woman sat in a chair beside the fireplace and a man stood behind her with his hand on her shoulder. She had pretty blonde hair and a face that was tired and sad even when she smiled. There were other people in the room too, moving around, drinking and eating and talking, but Angela couldn't hear what they said. It was like watching television with the sound turned off. Her mother did that sometimes, when she was balancing her checkbook.

Someone handed the sad-faced woman a present wrapped in shiny blue paper with a silver bow. She smiled in a way that pretended she was happy and opened the package. Her face went very still as she looked inside, and then began to change. First she looked shocked, almost frightened, and Angela wondered if there was a spider or a toad in the box. And then the most amazing joy flooded the woman's face, and her eyes were filled with wonder. Her skin seemed almost to glow. Everyone turned to watch as she reached inside the box.

"Come on, sweetheart." Her daddy placed his hand on Angela's shoulder. "Let's go before all the horse rides are taken."

"Daddy!" Angela whirled, clutching the snow globe to her chest. "Daddy, can I have this, please? Can I? I won't ask for anything else for Christmas, I promise, and Santa can take back the Barbie Dream House, but please, can I have it?"

"I'm sorry, Angel." The man from the counter knelt beside her and smiled gently as he took the globe from her hands. "It's not for sale."

"But . . ." She looked imploringly at her father as the man put the snow globe back on the shelf. "Daddy, there were people inside! They were laughing and talking and having a party! It was magic!"

The two men exchanged an indulgent look over her head, and the man from behind the counter said to her, "It certainly is, which is why it's not for sale." He had kind eyes, even though he had taken the snow globe from her. "We have to save some magic for the other boys and girls, don't we?"

She thought about that, and agreed reluctantly, "I guess so." Then, "What will happen to all the people living inside the ball?"

The kind man regarded her thoughtfully. "Why, they'll go on living their lives," he said, "just like you and I will."

Angela said, remembering the woman with the sad eyes, "I hope they have a happy Christmas."

The man smiled the kind of smile that made his whole face seem bigger. "Oh, I think they will," he said. "And I think you will too."

He looked again over her head to her father, still smiling, and the two men shook hands and wished each other Merry Christmas. Angela slipped her hand into her father's and the bell jangled again as they left the shop.

"Daddy," she said, glancing back at the golden square of light the window cast on the snow outside the shop, "how did that man know my name?"

Andrew glanced down at his daughter. "Your name?"

She nodded. "He called me Angel."

Andrew suppressed a smile. He might have told her that "angel" was a common nickname for sweet little girls like her, or that the clerk had probably heard Andrew call her that in the store. Instead he said easily, "Oh, I imagine that was just more magic."

She looked up at him, big eyed. "Like the people in the glass?"

He nodded somberly. "Exactly like that."

She said happily, "I love you, Daddy."

It was the best Christmas ever.

THE SHENANDOAH VALLEY

2015

You Are Cordially Invited to
Christmas at the Hummingbird House

Nestled in the heart of the Shenandoah Valley is the historic Hummingbird House Bed and Breakfast, your gateway to a fantasy Christmas that combines old-fashioned charm with modern elegance. Don't miss a holiday celebration you'll never forget!

The Hummingbird House is known for its attention to detail and creative approach to hospitality. Every guest is a treasure to us, and no effort is too great to assure that your stay at the Hummingbird House is a memorable one. Special events planned for the holiday weekend include:

* Wassail reception accompanied by the Dickens Christmas Carolers
* Evening sleigh ride and champagne supper under the stars
* Christmas tour of lights
* Reading and book signing by Geoffery Allen Windsor, author of *Miracles for the Modern Age*
* Tour of a local artisanal winery, including

a tasting and a bottle of complimentary wine
* Holiday cooking class with Bridget Tindale, owner of the Tasting Table Restaurant
* A private Christmas Day concert by the Killian Hills Boys Choir
* A special Christmas Eve chamber music performance by the Shenandoah Chamber Group
* Spa treatments including therapeutic wheatgrass wrap and couples massage
* A gala Christmas dinner prepared by one of the region's most acclaimed chefs [see menu online], accompanied by a selection of fine wines from our cellar.

Give yourself the gift of memories that will last a lifetime this holiday season. All inclusive Christmas packages begin at $3289 per couple for the weekend.

TWO

Full House

At the Hummingbird House Bed and Breakfast the first flake of snow had yet to fall, the first carol had yet to be sung, but the merry chaos of the upcoming Christmas extravaganza was everywhere. Paul Slater and Derrick Anderson, owners and proprietors of the Hummingbird House for almost six months now, had never done anything halfway in their lives, and their first Christmas in their new home was not to be the exception.

Their cozy office, designed to be a showcase for their collection of primitive antiques, was cluttered with boxes marked "fragile" and "perishable"; some going out, some coming in, some painstakingly transported from their storage unit just outside of DC where, upon selling both their in-town condo and their suburban Baltimore home, Paul and Derrick had consigned the boxes of Christmas ornaments they had collected over their thirty years together. Packing confetti escaped some of these boxes and littered the floor; brightly colored glass ornaments spilled from others.

A massive partners desk dominated the room,

and it was strewn with catalogues and design magazines, swatches of fabric and scraps of ribbon. Derrick's sketches for Christmas trees, holiday wreaths and seasonal mantel decor were scattered on both sides of the desk, along with design boards and sample books. The Hummingbird House had seven guest rooms, each with its own fireplace and private exterior door. Each room would have its own holiday theme, with a Christmas tree, mantel display, and two holiday wreaths—one for the door that opened onto the wraparound porch, and another for the door that opened into the hallway. There would be a communal tree in the gathering parlor, and one for the reception desk, and another in the dining room. The gardens would be decorated as well, so that guests could enjoy the twinkling lights from the glassed-in dining room—which, in the summer also served as a screened porch—or stroll the meandering paths at twilight with a glass of sherry or a cup of mulled wine. All of this required planning, preparation and design. They had been working on it since August.

It was now December tenth. Of course, all of the elaborate plans and decor would take some time to execute, and the first event of their holiday fantasy weekend—the wassail reception with costumed carolers—was scheduled to begin promptly at eight on December twenty-first. Unfortunately, the shortness of the approaching deadline had not yet occurred to either of the proprietors.

"Safe journey, Mrs. Feringer." Derrick air kissed each of the plump woman's powdered cheeks and beamed his good-bye as the last of their guests checked out that Monday morning. "Come again soon."

She sighed and gazed out the window where her husband waited in the Lexus, engine running, with the vista of neat winter lawn and big blue mountains in the background. "I wish we didn't have to leave. It's so peaceful here. Everything has been just perfect."

"Always a pleasure when the guests are as lovely as you," he assured her, squeezing her gloved hands with genuine sincerity. "What a shame you won't be with us for Christmas!"

"Well, the season is fast upon us, isn't it?" she agreed. "I'm sure you have an absolute wonderland planned, but family, you know. So many commitments."

"Maybe next year," Derrick suggested, and her eyes lit up with the possibility.

"Wouldn't that be a treat? I'll talk to Charles, I really will. Ta-ta, now!" The middle-aged woman was smiling in anticipation as she turned up her fur collar and went out into the cold bright morning.

Derrick was a man who truly loved his job—most of the time, anyway—and the only thing that gave him more pleasure than greeting the guests was seeing that blissful look in their eyes after they had enjoyed the hospitality of the Hummingbird House. He had owned a successful art gallery in Washington, DC, before retiring to the country with his partner Paul, although neither of them had any intention at the time of opening a bed and breakfast. They had more or less stumbled upon the Hummingbird House, made an impulsive decision, and were learning the business of innkeeping as they went along. There had been a few rough moments to start, but now everything seemed to be falling into place. And just in time for the holiday season.

Derrick was still smiling as he turned back to the reception desk, where he noticed their house-keeper Purline had left the morning's mail. He had asked her repeatedly to take the mail to the office, patiently explaining that leaving stacks of business mail out for guests to see completely destroyed the atmosphere of refined elegance they were trying to create, and for a while she had seemed to understand. Now it appeared she was slipping back into old habits. He sighed, picked up the stack, and started to call to her when the sound of the vacuum cleaner whined to life down the hall. Check-out was at 11:00 a.m. At precisely 11:05, Purline switched on the vacuum cleaner and kept it going without interruption for the next hour and a half. It would be pointless to try to talk to her now.

He glanced through the envelopes on his way to the office, and stopped when the return address on one of them caught his eye. "Oh my goodness," he whispered. "It's here." He slit open the envelope with his thumbnail, which only illustrated his excitement since he had a perfectly good ivory-handled letter opener with mother-of pearl inserts in his desk cubby, and he believed in doing things right. He pulled out the contents of the envelope, examined it with wondering, delighted eyes, and cried again, more loudly, "It's here!"

"It's here!" exclaimed Paul at the same time, coming around the corner with a large box in his arms.

And Harmony called from the office, "Gentlemen, it's here!" She came out of the office, beaming as she waved a sheet of paper fresh from the printer. "Our final reservation! We are officially booked for Christmas weekend!"

"The hummingbird ornaments from Hungary," Paul said excitedly, juggling the box to tug one of the exquisite little cut-glass birds from its wrapping. "They're magnificent!"

Paul Slater, the former syndicated style columnist for the *Washington Post* and best-selling author of several books on the same subject, was a tall, elegantly kept man in his sixties who managed to look flawlessly put together even in a rustic plaid shirt and deep green corduroy trousers. While the two men shared most of the general duties of running the B&B equally—only occasionally deferring to the opinion of their self-appointed general manager, Harmony—when it came to matters of decorating and style, Paul almost always had the last word. The handblown glass hummingbirds for the parlor Christmas tree were, according to Paul, an absolute must-have for their first Christmas at the Hummingbird House.

Derrick regarded them both with a triumphant, superior smile for a moment before declaring, "Our insurance check has arrived." And he brandished it in the air like a magician pulling a row of colorful scarves from his hat.

Paul's eyes grew big and he quickly—although very carefully—set the box of glass ornaments on the turned-leg table outside the office door. "Let me see that. Is it real?"

"Every last hard-earned penny," Derrick assured him.

Paul put on the glasses he wore on a chain around his neck, read the numbers and sank back against the wall in relief. "It's here," he said. "Our insurance check is here."

Before purchasing the Hummingbird House, Paul and Derrick had had a disastrous encounter with an unscrupulous contractor that resulted in their unfinished dream house falling into the unfinished pit of their dream swimming pool. While there was nothing to do about the parcel of land for which they now had no use, or about the contractor who had taken advantage of them and fled the state, it turned out that their insurance policy actually covered their losses on the unfinished house. Nonetheless, because the entire experience had been such a nightmare, neither of them had dared to believe they might ever recover anything . . . until now.

Peering over Paul's shoulder, Harmony smiled beneficently, looking far too pleased with herself. "There now, didn't I tell you? Didn't I say you would come into money before Christmas? When will you ever stop doubting me?"

Harmony was a dramatic-looking woman somewhere beyond the point of middle-age, tall, broad shouldered and big busted, with goldilocks curls, coarse skin and a flair for brightly colored caftans and outrageous jewelry. She liked to think of herself as "spiritually gifted," and in fact claimed it was her spirit guides who had led her to move semi-permanently into the Hummingbird House's fuchsia room. Paul and Derrick were still not entirely sure how they felt about this, but her idiosyncrasies were made a lot more palatable by the fact that she not only paid in full and on time every month, but had also assigned herself the role of part-time general manager of the B&B, freeing Paul and Derrick to do what they did best—provide their guests with a memorable vacation experience, complete in every detail. The fact that Harmony happened to be heiress to one of the largest hotel fortunes in the US did a great deal to plump up her credibility, of course. On the other hand, her tendency to fly off to Greece or Sri Lanka or Dubai on a moment's notice and be gone for weeks made her something less than a reliable GM.

She gave Paul's shoulder an affectionate pat and added, "And you were worried about building the spa! Everything comes together in perfect harmony when you listen to your inner truth."

Paul and Derrick exchanged a look and each of them decided, with the wisdom of experience, not to respond to that. The spa had been a point of contention between them since they'd bought the place, Derrick having envisioned something along the lines of the Golden Door Spa and Resort in Escondido, and Paul preferring more of a Roman Baths theme. As it turned out, none of the local builders were capable of executing either vision, and, having learned their lesson about hiring contractors from out of town, they compromised by extending one of the back rooms of the Hummingbird House and outfitting it with a hot tub, a steam room, and a massage room that overlooked the blissful serenity of the Appalachian mountains. Still, the cost was exorbitant, and none of their friends believed they could recoup their investment in a rural area like this.

As luck would have it, Harmony was also a

licensed massage therapist. Without her insistence, it was unlikely they would have gone through with the project. But they had to admit, the offer of a spa with couples massage had been the *pièce de résistance* in their Christmas package.

Both men momentarily gave their attention to Harmony. "Booked up," Paul said, and a slow and satisfied gleam lit his eyes. "We're booked up!"

He took the reservation form from Harmony's hand and admired it as he led the way to the office. "Dr. and Mrs. Bryce Phipps from Seattle, Washington," he read out loud. "They sound like a perfectly lovely couple."

"They're in what?" Derrick said, edging around Paul to study the reservation board that was mounted on the east wall of the office. "The plum room?"

Each room of the Hummingbird House was characterized by a brightly colored exterior door, each door a different color. The overall effect of those playfully painted doors on the rugged timber-frame lodge was both whimsical and ridiculous, and it was the most distinguishing visual feature of the inn—which, as Harmony pointed out, the camera loved. They had gotten more than one magazine feature already based on nothing but the doors.

The color theme of each door was carried into the room with tasteful decorative touches, and each room was named for its color. Derrick took a plum-colored magnet from his desk drawer, neatly printed the name "Phipps" on it, and placed it on the magnetic board in the column labeled "December 21–26." The row, filled with red, yellow, orange, emerald, blue, and chartreuse magnets, now was complete. Derrick gave a satisfied nod as he stepped back to admire it.

"A beautiful sight, isn't it?" he said.

"Oh dear, I keep telling you, you need to put Geoffery Allen Windsor in the blue room," Harmony said. "It's much more spiritual."

"But that would mean the Bartlett girls would be separated from their parents," Paul pointed out.

Harmony waved it away, her bracelets jangling. "They're fourteen and sixteen," she said. "They *want* to be separated from their parents."

"Mr. Bartlett specifically asked for a suite, and the melon and turquoise rooms are the only ones with a connecting door to accommodate them. We're doing their tree in magnolia blossoms and renaming it the Magnolia Suite for the duration." At Harmony's puzzled look he explained, rather annoyed, "Well, we could hardly decorate with melons, now could we? It was the best compromise we could come up with."

"We could move Mr. Windsor to the plum room," Derrick offered, "and put the Phippses in the yellow room. Purple is a spiritual color, isn't it?"

"No, no," Harmony said. "Plum is not the same energy at all, not at all."

"Too much red, I suppose," Derrick agreed thoughtfully. "I can see that."

"Mr. Windsor stays in the yellow room," Paul said firmly. "It has the best morning light, and he likes to write in the morning. And . . ." He finished entering the last of the reservation information into the computer and straightened up. "We've gone to far too much trouble designing the holiday themes for each room to start switching them around now."

"Very true." Derrick gave an adamant nod of his head. "Plum it is for the Phippses. Although . . ." He tilted his head toward Paul. "We have *got* to come up with better nomenclature for the yellow room. It's really more canary, don't you think?"

Paul shook his head. "No birds. We're not naming a room after a bird."

"Lemon?"

"Seriously?"

"Sunflower," declared Harmony. "The color is sunflower."

Paul and Derrick gave one another a considering look, but Harmony's attention was on the reservation board, her expression dreamy, as it often was. "Hildebrand, Matheson, Phipps, Bartlett, Windsor, Canon . . . Just names on a board, but they're going to be part of your family for the holidays. Don't you wonder who they are? What their stories are?"

"Oh, we know most of them already," Paul

assured her cheerily. "Bryce Phipps is a rather prominent surgeon, according to his online bio, and his wife is in interior design, although it seems to be mostly a hobby these days." He glanced back at the computer, scrolled down a page, and added, "They've been married almost forty years, no children. She was on the board of the San Francisco Symphony 2005 to 2008, and they're both major sponsors of the theater, which will certainly give them something to talk about with Mr. Canon, who's retired from Pinnacle Records. *His* wife is a fanatical gardener—second wife, I understand—and mad about specialty roses, which is why, you understand, they *must* be in the rose room."

"We're decorating their tree with living roses," explained Derrick. "Exquisite."

"And of course," Paul went on, "everyone knows Mr. Windsor, who is one of only two of our single guests. One might dare hope for a little holiday romance to blossom, except the other single guest is well past eighty years old, Mrs. Hildebrand."

"Delightful to talk to on the phone," Derrick put in, "very spry, a world traveler. She was the executive editor of *Seasons Magazine* until she retired last year. Starts every morning with a shot of espresso, ends every day with scotch on the rocks."

"The Mathesons are on their honeymoon,

although I gather this is only one of many stops. Carl Bartlett is a senior vice president with Apricot Foods, and his wife Leona is an attorney with a nonprofit in Richmond, mostly part time, I believe, just to keep her hand in. They both are quite well known in the Richmond social scene, I understand. I can't say I know much more about them, but the gentleman seemed quite nice on the phone, wants to give his girls an old-fashioned Christmas, which is exactly what we're offering. As for everything else, we'll know soon enough, won't we? And of course, we already know they all have one thing in common—they all have excellent taste."

"As demonstrated by the fact that they're spending their holidays with us," agreed Derrick.

Harmony looked from one to the other of them in bemusement. "How on earth do you know all of this?"

"Well," replied Paul as though the answer should be obvious, "that's our job, isn't it?"

Harmony laughed and looped an arm through each of theirs as they moved back out into the hallway. "Well, congratulations, boys! You're booked up for your first holiday in the business! Quite an accomplishment."

"That ad we placed in *Travel and Leisure* was pure genius," agreed Derrick, "if I do say so myself."

"Disguising it as an invitation was beyond

brilliant," pointed out Paul, eyebrow raised, "if I do say so myself."

"And don't forget all the free publicity you got with your grand opening," added Harmony, "which was nothing but the spirits at work."

Paul and Derrick exchanged another look. "Harmony," said Paul, who, generally speaking, was known to manage Harmony with a much firmer hand than Derrick, "if you're building up to that whole issue of painting cherubs on the ceiling of the massage room again, I'm afraid our decision on that is final."

"Not," Derrick added quickly, "that it isn't a perfectly lovely idea." He ignored the warning look Paul cast him and plunged on, "It's just that, seriously, who would see them? I mean, one's eyes are generally facing the floor during a massage, or closed entirely, am I right? Not to mention that finding a competent muralist this far from civilization is next to impossible."

"Angels, my darlings, *angels,* not cherubs," Harmony said with a confident smile on her face; never a good sign. "And don't you worry about a thing. I'll take care of it all when I return."

Derrick said, "Return from where?"

And Paul added suspiciously, "When you return from town, right? When you return from Christmas shopping? When . . ."

"When I return from India in the new year!" she announced triumphantly, her eyes shining. "When

I return transformed by six weeks of meditation with one of the most acclaimed spiritual teachers of our time! I leave tomorrow. Aren't you thrilled for me?"

As one, the two men stepped away from her, regarding her with identical expressions of shock and disbelief. "You can't be serious," Paul said.

"But our Christmas extravaganza!" Derrick cried.

"We've promised massages to fourteen extremely well-paying guests . . ."

"We only built the spa because you assured us you could accommodate the traffic . . ."

"All right," Paul said, drawing a deep and pained breath. "I know we never talked about compensation, but we're willing to pay . . ." He darted a quick glance at Derrick for confirmation. "Once and again the hourly rate. For the holiday season only," he was quick to add.

Harmony was, to put it bluntly, a rather homely woman, but when she laughed that light, tinkling laugh of hers, as she did now, her face was transformed into something almost lovely. "Boys, boys, I don't want your money," she said with a wave of her arm that sent two dozen silver bracelets jangling. "I've got plenty of my own. But a place at the ashram? There's a waiting list two years long! Why, if that poor old professor from Illinois hadn't had a heart attack—

may God rest his soul—I'd still be waiting!"

"And we'd have a massage therapist," Derrick pointed out, a little desperately.

Again she waved it away, bracelets tinkling like jingle bells. "Not to worry, I've already arranged for a perfectly marvelous couple to take over for me. They do amazing chakra work, and he's board-certified in reflexology. Our guests will adore them."

Cautiously, Derrick relaxed. "Well, I suppose if you've made the arrangements . . ."

But Paul was less forgiving. "Honestly, Harmony, this is most inconsiderate," he said, exasperated. "We were counting on you."

She beamed at him and gave his arm a reassuring pat. "You can always count on me, darling. I've checked off everything on my project board, haven't I? Horse-drawn sleighs and drivers are all lined up, the window van for the tour of lights will be here promptly at six on the twenty-third, chamber music, boys' choir, carolers all set to perform. Now I'm off to pack. And don't you worry about those angels," she added over her shoulder. "I'll get it all taken care of."

She turned down the corridor that led to her room, caftan fluttering.

Purline approached from the opposite hall-way, ponytail swinging, gum snapping, vacuum cleaner clattering behind her. She was somewhere between eighteen and thirty—neither man had ever had the courage to ask her age—dressed today in bright red leggings, shearling-lined moccasins and a green "Go Elf Yourself" tee shirt. She was something of a challenge, it was true, but she went through the place like a cleaning tornado, and was more than just a little competent in the kitchen. For a good cook and someone who sprinkled the sheets with orange water before ironing them, the men could put up with a lot.

"Y'all ain't planning on holing up in that office, are you?" she called out. "I need to get in there and clean."

Paul protectively picked up the box of glass ornaments from the hall table. "Not now, Purline," he said. "We have all our plans and samples set out just where we want them, and if you move anything we'll never find them again."

"You've been saying that for two weeks," she replied. "You're gonna get mice if you're not careful."

Derrick looked alarmed, but Paul assured him, "We won't get mice." For a moment he looked a little unsure of himself, and then recovered his composure with a frown. "Why don't you finish the guest rooms first and come back this afternoon, Purline?" he said. "We have a lot to take care of this morning."

Purline craned her neck to peer around him into the office. "My cousin left a cheese sand-

35

wich on her desk one night," she said. "Got up the next morning to find a mouse'd had babies in her top drawer, right on top of her income tax forms."

Derrick's eyes flew wide, but Paul said, "Not now, Purline. We have a full house for Christmas, and we just found out Harmony isn't even going to be here."

Purline returned a skeptical look. "You boys don't know when to count your blessings, do you?" She made no secret of the fact that there was no love lost between Harmony and herself. Then she frowned, her expression turning suspicious. "Full house, huh? I hope that don't mean you expect me to work on Christmas Day."

Paul looked insulted. "Purline, don't be ridiculous! We know you have little ones at home. The magic of Christmas morning, and all of that."

"We'd never dream of asking you to come in on Christmas," Derrick added earnestly, "until after noon."

"At time and a half," added Paul quickly.

The corners of her mouth turned down as she regarded them. "Well, I guess I can't leave you with a full house," she decided at last. "I'll come in and change the sheets and clean the bathrooms, but that's it."

"Thank you, Purline," Derrick said.

"Our guests deserve clean sheets on Christmas Day," Paul insisted gravely, and she considered this.

"I guess," she agreed, and then added, "but I'm not staying more than an hour or two. We're all going over to my granny's for Christmas dinner and more present-opening, and my husband Bill always plays Santa Claus." She paused and glanced around. "Kinda sad, though, when you think about it, ain't it?"

Paul's expression clearly showed he was having trouble following her thoughts. "What is?"

She said, "All these people, coming in from all over the country, with nothing better to do than spend Christmas with you-all. Makes you wonder where their grannies are, don't it?"

Paul and Derrick looked equally startled and confused, clearly having never considered this before. But before either of them could form an answer, or even think of one, Purline shrugged it off with a snap of her gum.

"Anyhows," she said, "what I wanted to ask you was what're you going to do with all them boxes of flowers and stuff still sitting on the back porch in the cold where the UPS man left them. Didn't you say that woman was in charge of the decorations?" *That woman* was Purline's preferred way of referring to Harmony.

"The poinsettias and evergreen garlands," Paul explained to Derrick. "I was so excited when I saw the boxes of ornaments I forgot about them. We'd probably better get them into the storeroom. And let's not forget to leave a *huge* tip for the UPS driver this Christmas."

Derrick looked uneasy. "That's right," he said, glancing back toward Harmony's room. "Harmony was in charge of the floral decor. I assumed that meant actually arranging everything, not just ordering it."

"We always had a crew do the decorating at home," Paul remembered, sounding a little concerned himself. Sometimes they still referred to their former house in the suburbs—and, in fact, their former condo in Washington—as "home."

"I didn't see 'hire a decorating crew' on Harmony's project board," Derrick said.

Paul looked worried. "I didn't see it on anybody's board."

"And that's another thing," Purline said, oblivious. "I wish to high heaven somebody would explain to me why you've got to order pine branches from some fancy florist in Washington, DC, when you're sitting smack dab in the middle of a forest, practically."

"Well, Purline, it's really not quite that simple," Paul started to explain in a faintly condescending tone, but she waved him away.

"Whatever," she said. "Just go on and get them things off the porch so I can get out there and sweep. By the way," she added, "just so you know,

38

I'll be bringing the kids with me tomorrow. Don't worry, I'll keep them out of the office."

"Kids?" Derrick echoed. "Your kids?"

And Paul added quickly, "Purline, I'm afraid that's simply not appropriate . . ."

"No children under twelve are allowed at the Hummingbird House," Derrick put in. "It clearly states so in our policy. No pets, no smoking, no children under twelve."

Purline snapped her gum. "My kids don't smoke."

"Purline, seriously . . ."

"It's just till my mama gets back from Arizona," she interrupted impatiently. "You won't even know they're here."

"Your mother?" Derrick seemed to be able to do little more than parrot her words. The thought of children running amuck in the Hummingbird House had completely stripped him of his nerve.

"She usually takes care of them while they're out of school," Purline explained, "but my sister's having gallbladder surgery so she had to go out and stay with her, didn't she? It being Christmas and all. Speaking of Christmas, when are you all going to put up your tree?"

"Trees," corrected Paul. "The Hummingbird House will have multiple trees on display. Each room will be a different vignette, which is another reason we simply can't have children . . ."

"Well, I'd get to it if I was you," she said. "Fifteen days till Christmas and all. I know a place you can cut your own for twenty dollars, any size. Just let me know." She grasped the handle of the vacuum cleaner and started to turn back the way she had come, then caught sight of the check that was still in Derrick's hand. She peered closer. "Lord have mercy," she said, "just look at all those commas. You folks really *don't* know when to count your blessings, do you? I'll be back after lunch," she added, straightening up, "and I'm cleaning that office whether you like it or not."

The two men stood in the corridor for a moment after she was gone, Derrick gazing down rather guiltily at the check in his hand, and Paul staring at Derrick. Paul said, "Did you hear what she said?"

Derrick nodded. "She's right. We really do need to stop and count our blessings."

"No," Paul said impatiently. "Not that. Christmas is only fifteen days away!"

Derrick lifted his eyes slowly to Paul's as understanding dawned. "Oh good heavens," he said. "We haven't put up a single vignette."

"And if Harmony's not going to be here to hang the garland and arrange the flowers . . ."

"Not to mention the tablescapes . . ."

"Or the outdoor lighting . . ."

"Or the Christmas trees!" Derrick took a single

deep sobering breath. "We have got to get busy," he said.

"We have to get help," clarified Paul.

Derrick gave a decisive nod. "We have to talk to the girls," he said.

THREE

The Sunflower Room

Miracles," intoned Geoffery Allen Windsor, "are usually identified as supernatural events, divine intervention on the behalf of human beings in crisis. And as you've seen from some of the examples in this book, this is very often the case. But another way to define a miracle is when you find exactly what you need when you need it. If you look at it like that, I think you'll start to see miracles all around you, every single day."

He took off his glasses, looking over the lectern at the small clutch of people gathered in the back room of the bookstore. He was an aging, slightly stooped-shouldered man with thinning hair who had said those same words a thousand times, taken off his glasses just like that a thousand times, and smiled that same smile a thousand times before. "Thank you for coming. Each and every one of you is certainly a miracle in my life. I'll be happy to sign copies or answer any questions you have."

A handful of people came up to ask him to sign copies—most of them purchased from a used bookstore, he couldn't help but notice—or to tell him their own amazing story of the sister whose ten-pound tumor disappeared or the dog who came back home after five years. He listened with a polite smile and glazed-over eyes, and signed his name with a simple "Happy holidays" inscription. "I love the story of the angel at the Twin Towers," one plump, middle-aged woman confided. There was always at least one. "Do you think it really happened?" He told her, as he always did, that he only collected the stories, he hadn't witnessed them, but that he believed all things were possible with faith.

In his line of work, it was important to be able to tell a good lie.

Eventually the room cleared and he walked out with Bobbie, who was waiting at the back of the room dying for a smoke. He knew he should stop to thank the store manager, but she was busy at one of the registers, ringing up wrapping paper and stereo headphones and DVDs of the latest zombie apocalypse movie. Besides, thank her for what? She hadn't sold a single copy of his book, although why that should surprise him he didn't know. The last things bookstores were interested in selling these days were books.

He pulled on his coat and gloves and he and Bobbie pushed out into the dull gray light of a crowded mall parking lot just outside of Little Rock, Arkansas. Bobbie snatched a pack of cigarettes from the pocket of her stylish black leather coat and lit up almost before the door closed behind them.

"You're the last person in America who still smokes," he observed.

She blew out a long satisfied stream of gray smoke. "At least I'll be remembered for something."

He shot her a dark look and she patted his arm in casual reassurance. "Not that you're not enough to be remembered for, darling. After all, thirty-six weeks on the *Times* list is nothing to be sneezed at."

"That was six years ago."

"Well." She inhaled deeply and blew out smoke. "There's that."

He nodded toward the coffee kiosk that was arranged beneath a cluster of naked Japanese maples strung with white lights just outside the entrance to J.C. Penney, and they turned their steps in that direction. "So let's have it," he said. "You didn't come all the way out here just to listen to that speech again."

Bobbie Banks had been Geoffery's representative at the prestigious Leeman Literary Agency for over ten years. In the beginning, she had been there to help kick off every book tour and personal appearance, and had made it a point to be in the audience when he appeared on Oprah or Regis and Kelly. And why shouldn't she have been? He was making her—not to mention the agency—a fortune. These days he was lucky to get her on the phone once or twice a year, and he knew for a fact that the only reason she had been at the reading today was because she was in town for the same writer's conference he was. He had been invited to be on a panel about writing nonfiction; she was scouting for new clients.

They took two paper cups of coffee and sat on an iron bench beneath the display of white lights. A gaggle of teenage girls in boots and colorful striped scarves walked past, giggling and texting and sharing Instagram photos on their phones. Bobbie blew out a last stream of smoke and stubbed out the cigarette on the side of the bench. "It's not that I didn't try, darling, you know that. But the publisher has decided not to go with the second Miracle book. You surely can't be surprised. They feel the material has run its course and the audience just isn't what it used to be. The entire book industry isn't what it used to be, you know that. Hell, *I'm* not what I used to be."

Geoffery sipped his coffee and said nothing. Bobbie lit another cigarette.

"What I need from you," she said, blowing out smoke, "is something new, fresh, dynamic. Something I can get excited about. I mean, this stuff was hot back in oh-nine when the country was in a nosedive and everybody was running scared, but we've moved on since then. Do you know what I mean?"

He nodded slowly, taking another sip of his

coffee. "It's a lot easier to sell hope during a recession."

"Precisely! But we're all driving new cars now, everybody's back to work, and nobody's interested in that sentimental drivel these days." She cast a quick look at him. "Sorry, darling, I don't mean to hurt your feelings. You know what I mean."

He gave a small grunt of mirthless laughter. "Of course I do. I'm the one who has to *read* that sentimental drivel to old ladies in the backs of bookstores and blog about that sentimental drivel three times a week and talk about that sentimental drivel ad nauseum every time somebody asks me out to dinner. And I'll tell you something else." He drank from his cup. "There was no damn angel at the Twin Towers."

She nodded her understanding and drew on the cigarette, giving his knee a single reassuring pat. "As long as we're on the same page."

She smoked in silence for a moment, and he sipped his coffee. "What you need is a good celebrity exposé, or a true crime. They're short-lived, but big bucks. I could get you six figures today for a behind-the-scenes exclusive with a mass murderer."

"I don't know any mass murderers."

"God knows there're enough of them to choose from."

"Still don't know any of them."

She glanced at him. "Well, you didn't know any-one who'd ever seen an angel until you started looking, did you?"

"Still don't."

"Just think about it."

"I will." He took another sip of his coffee. "God knows I'm not going to be able to live off what I'm making much longer."

She snorted laughter, blowing smoke through her nose. "Baby, I *already* can't live off what you're making."

They shared a smile, and she stubbed out her cigarette. "Well, I've got to get back. I'm inter-viewing five more wannabes this afternoon, and I haven't been able to make myself read even one of their proposals. Talk about your miracles. That's what it would be if I can find a semiliterate sentence in that pile of dreck. Walk me to the shuttle?"

"Sure." He stood. "I guess I'll head back to the hotel, too. I think there's an episode of *Castle* on television this afternoon that I haven't seen, and happy hour starts in the Kingfisher room at 4:00. They have free pigs-in-a-blanket."

She looped her arm through his, and they walked back toward the parking lot, her high-heeled boots clicking on the sidewalk. "What are your plans for the holidays?"

"Actually, I'm doing a reading at a B and B in Virginia. Four days, five nights in the middle of the woods, stargazing by night, reading beside the fire during the day. And I only have to work for one afternoon."

She wrinkled her nose. "Sounds ghastly."

"It was that or an inside, below-decks, eight-by-ten cabin on a cruise to the Bahamas, seven days of making nice with eighteen hundred people, three readings and one night of leading the conga line. It seemed to me there was less chance of listeria at the B and B, and besides, they're offering a stipend. It's Paul Slater's place," he added. "You remember him, from the *Washington Post*?"

"Oh, so that's what he's doing now. Come to think of it, I do seem to recall reading he'd bought a place in the country after he left the *Post*. Now, there's a man who knows how to make money hand over fist. Three best-sellers, three years in a row? Please. And I still have his coffee-table book. Do me a favor, will you?" She stopped and plucked a business card out of a side pocket in her purse. "Give him my card. Ask if he's happy with his representation."

Geoffery hesitated, then took the card with a resigned quirk of his lips and tucked it into his pocket. "Right."

They edged past a Christmas topiary display outside the Sears entrance, where animated elves tossed an endless supply of artificial snowflakes over a garden of lighted trees. It seemed to be a popular place for mothers with children in strollers to stop and point and make baby talk.

Geoffery asked politely, "So what are you doing for the holidays?"

She lit another cigarette and waved away the smoke. "Oh, please. I lost my religion decades ago, and I'm a lot happier for it. I don't even celebrate Chanukah any more. Thought about the Hamptons, but they're dead this time of year. Probably I'll just watch the parade from my window and catch up on some work. Ah, screw the parade. It's just a bunch of freaky little men in worn-out elf costumes dancing around, anyway. I mean seriously, I ask you, aren't we all tired of Christmas by December twenty-fifth anyway?"

"Bobbie, can I ask you something?"

He stopped and looked at her seriously. She started to take another drag on the cigarette, then changed her mind, waiting.

Geoffery said, "There's never been a publisher in the history of the world who rejected a book because it was based on a tried and true formula. Why did they really turn down the second book?"

Bobbie dropped the cigarette and crushed it with the toe of her boot. She returned a steady gaze to him. "It's you, Geoffery," she said. "Your writing. They thought it felt like you were phoning it in, rehashing old stuff. What made the first book so powerful was the way you told it, the way you convinced us, the way you, I don't know, *cared*. Hell, you almost had me converting once or twice." She tried for a smile and failed. "But when Liz died," she went on, "I saw something go out of you. I kept expecting it to come back, but it never did. So the truth is . . . maybe this isn't your genre anymore. Things change, you know?"

For a long moment, he didn't reply. And then he said, quietly, "Yeah. I know."

They walked back to the shuttle without speaking.

FOUR

Ladybugs and Angel Cakes

Paul and Derrick's friendship with Bridget, Cici and Lindsay dated back to the time they had all lived on Huntington Lane, a tony neighborhood in the suburbs of Baltimore. Between the five of them, they'd practically run the Homeowner's Association, the Gardens and Beautification Committee, and the Thursday Night Supper Club. They'd gone to the theater together, taken the train into Washington for shopping trips and gallery openings together, and every autumn they made a sojourn into the country to pick apples together. At least the ladies picked apples; Paul and Derrick preferred to have their baskets filled by professionals and waiting for them at the gift shop at the end of the day. They took turns trying to outdo each other by giving the best parties in town, and they *always* celebrated Christmas together.

Paul and Derrick had been at first appalled, then secretly envious, when the three ladies decided to abandon suburbia, consolidate their resources, and buy an old mansion in the Shenandoah Valley together. They'd called the place Ladybug Farm, and spent the next year refurbishing the interior, restoring gardens and shoring up outbuildings. By the time Paul and Derrick made their own move to the country several years later, the ladies had even revitalized the vineyard and had begun operating a winery. Cici's daughter Lori had married Bridget's son Kevin, and the two of them had moved into the big old house. Lindsay had adopted a teenage boy, Noah, who was now a Marine stationed in Washington, DC, and had married Dominic Duponcier, the vineyard manager. What had begun as a simple house restoration had turned into a big, colorful, noisy, mismatched family.

Ladybug Farm was twenty minutes down the highway from the Hummingbird House, and Paul and Derrick visited often—most often, as they both were painfully aware, when they needed help of some sort. Their friends were generous with their advice and their time, not to mention their homemade cookies and pies, and the two men tried very hard not to take advantage of them. But somehow they always suspected they were. This time, at least, they had each had the presence of mind to grab a poinsettia from one of the boxes on the back porch, hoping that might make this seem like more of a social call than yet another imposition upon the ladies' collective good nature.

The Ladybug Farm sign at the end of the drive was already decorated with red bows and bright holly bouquets, and someone had festooned the winery sign with cedar swags and more red bows. The drive that led to the winery was lined on either side by quaint split-rail fences, and these, too, were lushly adorned with the bounty of nature—cedar boughs and pine cones—accented by more red velvet bows. Above the door of the winery was a huge grapevine wreath highlighted by a single giant red bow and lined with white lights. As Paul stopped the car in the circular drive in front of the house, they noted wreaths on every window, and swaths of bow-studded garland looping the railing of the wraparound porch. More garland—as well as lights, no doubt—climbed each of the white columns, draping artfully over the arch of the front door. The front door displayed one of the most elaborate holiday wreaths either of them had ever seen, complete with dried hydrangeas in breathtaking hues of lavender and pink, silver ribbon, miniature birds, and tastefully arranged glass spheres in shades of pink and purple.

Paul turned off the engine and looked uncomfortably at Derrick. "I don't know about you," he said, "but I feel a bit like a beggar at the feast."

"And we haven't even gone inside," agreed Derrick glumly.

The moment they started to open their doors a black and white terror in the form of a border collie charged around the corner of the house, teeth bared, voice raging, and flung himself at their front right tire. They closed the doors and waited, as anyone who had ever visited Ladybug Farm was trained to do, for someone to come along to control the beast. That someone was Lori, who came from the back in jeans, scuffed green rain boots, and a quilted red vest over a flannel shirt. Her copper curls escaped a knit cap with yellow yarn braids, and she wore matching yellow knit gloves. Seeing her, Paul could not prevent a great sigh.

"Once she was a fashion diva," he said.

"At least the gloves match the hat," Derrick offered, although he, too, looked pained.

Lori, struggling with the contents of a gallon bucket, planted it by the corner of the porch and rushed forward, shouting, "Rebel, no!"

She grabbed the dog by the collar and dragged him away from the car, calling happily, "Hi, Uncle Derrick! Uncle Paul! What'd you bring me?"

They held up the poinsettias hopefully. "Flowers?" Paul called back through his barely opened window.

She wrinkled her nose. "A Victoria's Secret gift card would be better."

Paul said, "Love you, precious!"

She grinned. "Love you back!" She hauled the dog away from the car and added, "Everybody's in the kitchen. Except Dominic, who's in the winery, and Kev, who's at school." Her husband,

Kevin, taught business at the community college while working on his PhD from UVA. In his spare time, he also helped run the winery. She gave the dog a swat on the bottom that sent him racing off toward the meadows and said, "Got to feed the chickens. Merry Christmas!"

"Merry Christmas to you, sweetie!" They both called back, but waited until she was gone and the dog was well out of sight before they got out of the car.

They walked around the wide porch to the kitchen door. It was wrapped like a present in red and green calico and tied with an enormous red velvet bow—Lori's idea, no doubt, who could always be counted on for a whimsical touch. A garland of cedar boughs outlined the door frame, decorated with tiny silver bows and sparkling red, lime green and silver Christmas balls. Rustic milk cans filled with bright red berries and greenery decorated with more of the red, silver and lime green ornaments flanked the door, and beside the steps there was a stack of boxes wrapped in more colorful calico and tied with bright floppy bows, as though Santa had just dropped them off. Lori, again. The white wicker table where, during the warmer months, the ladies often had breakfast, was now decorated with a red and green plaid tablecloth lightly shot through with silver, and bright red cushions adorned the chairs. There were playful felt Santa placemats and a runner of cedar boughs studded with more red, green and silver balls. Two white pillar candles stood on that bed of greenery, flanking a centerpiece of—what else?—red poinsettias.

"A bit over the top, don't you think?" Derrick murmured, and Paul shifted his gaze upward in silent agreement.

"It's not as though *they* have every room booked with paying guests who are coming from all over the country expecting the quintessential holiday experience," he said. "Although," he admitted reluctantly as he gave the table decor a closer look, "that really is quite charming in its own Ladybug Farm way."

Clutching their poinsettias before them like badges of honor, they approached the door where, from the kitchen beyond, they could hear the voices of women raised in a discussion which, while it might not be described as heated, was certainly not conversational. Paul glanced at Derrick. Derrick gave an uncertain shrug. Paul knocked on the door and then pushed it open.

The big country kitchen was in a state of mild chaos, and not necessarily the cheerful, busy kind that is welcome during the holidays. Cookbooks, recipe cards and manila folders filled with stained and dog-eared magazine clippings were scattered across the soapstone island that dominated the room. Cici, a tall, athletic-looking woman with deeply freckled skin and spikes of honey-blonde hair spilling from a messy topknot, was on a ladder pulling things out of the top cabinets. Bridget, as neat as a pin in her platinum bob, gray slouch boots and a bright Christmas apron over her crisp white shirt and black jeans, looked very close to exasperation as she thumbed through the contents of the manila folders on the counter. Ida Mae, their aged and intractable housekeeper, looked like a ferocious elf in clunky work boots, green-and-white knee socks, and a long red cardigan over a gray wool dress. Her mouth was set grimly as she pulled open drawers, scrambled though them, and slammed them shut again.

Bridget exclaimed impatiently, "Honestly, Ida Mae, if I had seen it, don't you think I'd tell you? I really don't know what you expect me to do!"

And Cici added, "What makes you think it would still be here after forty years, anyway? Somebody probably threw it away when they cleaned out the house to put it up for sale."

"*I'm* the one that cleaned out the house," Ida Mae replied testily, her iron gray curls bobbing with repressed frustration as she slammed shut another door. "And I ain't about to throw away something that valuable. Do I look like a fool to you?"

Paul and Derrick exchanged another uncertain look, but it was too late to back out now. "Yoo-hoo!" Paul sang out. "Company!"

Cici looked down from the ladder, her

expression delighted and surprised. "Boys! I didn't know you were coming over!"

Bridget's expression was intensely relieved as she opened her arms to embrace them. "How wonderful to see you!"

Ida Mae just scowled at them. But from her, it was a warm welcome.

There were quick hugs between Cici and Bridget and the two men, while Ida Mae demanded, "You all staying to eat?"

"No, ma'am," Derrick assured her quickly, and thrust his ivory-colored poinsettia at her with a smile. "We just stopped by to bring you this and wish you happy holidays."

"A whole shipment of them arrived this morning," Paul added, presenting his pale pink-colored plant to Bridget. "Naturally we thought of you."

"How sweet!" Bridget exclaimed. "And what lovely colors!"

"Ivory and blush," Derrick said. "Our theme for the entrance and dining room."

"Right pretty," admitted Ida Mae gruffly, holding the plant out to examine it. "Of course, I'm partial to red myself."

She shuffled off to place the plant in the big bay window on the other side of the room, her steel-toed boots clacking on the brick floor. Bridget placed her plant in the center of the hickory table that sat beside the raised fireplace. A fire crackled merrily in the grate beneath a colorful mantel display featuring a wooden sleigh carrying loads of Christmas presents and a string of painted alphabet blocks spelling out "Merry Christmas." The table was set, naturally, with red and green Fiestaware and casual red plaid napkins.

"Do stay for lunch," Bridget urged. "I think we have some Brunswick stew in the freezer." She knew it was Paul's favorite.

"Then you have to stay," Cici said. "Otherwise, all we're having is crackers and tomato soup. From a can." She made a face as she gestured around the kitchen. "We've been a little distracted."

Lindsay pushed through the swinging door then, the sleeves of her sweatshirt pushed up, smudges of dust on the knees of her jeans and across her forehead. There were a few stray cobwebs clinging to her auburn ponytail, which she plucked away in annoyance. "I give up," she declared. "I've opened every box in that attic and . . ." She broke off with a smile as she noticed Paul and Derrick. "Hi, guys! What brings you over?"

"They're staying for lunch," Cici said.

Derrick protested, "No, really, we can't."

And Paul said, "What on earth are you looking for?"

"Ida Mae lost a recipe," Bridget replied.

"She's been driving us crazy about it for the last week," added Cici.

Derrick looked surprised as he turned to Ida Mae. "Ida Mae, I've never known you to even use a recipe."

"Precisely," declared Lindsay.

Ida Mae gave Lindsay a dark look. "Shows what you know, Missy. Everything starts with a recipe."

"But I'd think you'd have them all memorized by now," Paul said.

"She hasn't made it in forty years," confided Cici.

"That ain't got nothing to do with it," Ida Mae said harshly. She took a stew pot out of the cabinet and clattered it down on the stove. "Some recipes you can mess with, some you can't. This here's the Christmas Angel Cake. It's only got seven ingredients, and if you don't get 'em just right, the angel won't come. And I promised to take it to the church supper Christmas Eve, so all I can say is y'all better keep on huntin'."

Bridget gave a small shrug of her shoulders and a roll of her eyes.

"Did you try an Internet search?" Paul suggested helpfully.

"First thing," Lindsay assured him.

"Dozens of hits," Cici said. "None of them was the right one."

"I keep tryin' to tell you," Ida Mae said from across the room, "there wasn't no dad-blamed Internet when this here recipe was invented."

Again Bridget rolled her eyes, and started

gathering up the cookbooks and papers strewn across the island.

Ida Mae said, "I'm starting my cornbread. If y'all ain't stayin', speak up before I crack the eggs."

Paul demurred, "Well, if you insist . . ."

But Derrick interrupted firmly, albeit with genuine regret, "As much as we'd love to, we really must fly. 'Tis the season, and all that. We really just wanted to drop off the poinsettias, and to, um . . ." He cast an urgent look at Paul for help.

Paul, still struggling with his disappointment over missing lunch, supplied, "And to tell you the good news. We got our insurance check. *And* we're all booked up for Christmas weekend!"

"That's fabulous, guys!"

"Congratulations!"

Bridget clapped her hands together happily. "That means my cooking class will be full! What fun!"

"We thought we'd celebrate with an impromptu tree-trimming party tomorrow afternoon," added Derrick on an inspiration. "We want you all to come. Dominic and the kids, too."

"Especially Dominic," said Paul. "He has such a way with lights and ladders and such."

"Nothing fancy," Derrick hurried on, "just eggnog and cookies, maybe a few light hors d'ouevres . . ."

But already the women were shaking their

heads. "Sounds wonderful," Lindsay said, "and you know we love your parties, but we have a full house for Christmas too! Dominic's children are coming . . ."

"And Katie and her husband are bringing the twins," added Bridget happily. "It's the first time the whole family will be together for Christmas in four years!"

"Noah can't get leave for the whole weekend," Lindsay said, "but he's driving down Christmas afternoon. The whole great big crazy blended family is going to be all together under one roof. Makes this house seem a little small, if you can believe it."

"It's going to be great," said Cici, eyes shining. "I love a full table for Christmas dinner. But we still have a lot of work to do before they get here."

"There is no way I can get away tomorrow, or any time before Christmas," Bridget assured him. "Ida Mae and I haven't even started cooking yet. We've got at least six dozen cookies to make, four or five casseroles, and I don't know how many pies and cakes . . ."

"You can forget about me baking any cakes until I find my recipe," Ida Mae warned dourly, "and that's just a plain fact. I ain't in a baking mood."

"And I've got to start rearranging the guest rooms," Cici said, "and cleaning the carpets and the drapes."

"Lori and Kevin promised to help me paint the

downstairs sewing room and carry some of the furniture down from the attic so we can use it as an extra bedroom," Lindsay went on. "And Dominic is driving down to Richmond tomorrow to look for a new bottler, so he can't help. Gosh, it's an awful lot of fun to have company, but a lot of trouble too. I don't know how you boys do it every day of the year!"

Then Cici looked at them suspiciously. "Wait. Do you mean to tell me you haven't even decorated your tree yet?"

Paul gave a light dismissing laugh. "Trees, darling, trees! We have dozens of them. But of course we wanted to save a little of the fun to share with you."

Cici looked relieved, though not entirely convinced. "I've got all the fun I can handle, thanks. But I will miss your eggnog."

"Drop by anytime," Derrick replied easily. "We'll always have a cup for you."

The moment threatened to become awkward as they all just stood there smiling at each other, the ladies clearly anxious to get back to work while Paul and Derrick lingered, trying to find a way to bring up their desperate need for several pairs of helping hands without sounding pathetic, or even worse, duplicitous.

Ida Mae rattled pots and pans meaningfully at the stove, prompting Derrick into action. "Well, my lovelies, off we go!" he declared heartily, blowing a collective kiss to them while Paul just stared at him with an accusing look. He grabbed Paul's arm and turned to the door. Then, on an inspiration, glanced back. "By the way," he said, "meant to mention that we're looking for someone to help out with chores for the next few weeks. Filling wood boxes, keeping the walk swept, that sort of thing. So if you know anyone in need of a little holiday cash, send him our way. Maybe your man Farley?"

Farley was the local handyman, and practically a fixture around Ladybug Farm. Paul shot an admiring and grateful look at Derrick, which faded quickly as Bridget said, "Oh, I don't think Farley would be much help. He's been laid up with a slipped disc all month. That reminds me, Ida Mae, we need to fix up a basket for him. He loves my chess pie. Do we have enough eggs?"

She opened the refrigerator door to check while Ida Mae groused about not having all day to make a chess pie. Cici said with a shrug, "Everybody's pretty busy this time of year, but I'll let you know if I hear about anyone."

"If you hear about anyone," Lindsay told her, "send him to me to paint the sewing room." Then she grinned at the two men. "You know something, guys? I'm so proud of the way you've settled in and taken over running the B and B. When you first started you were over here every minute with some crisis or another, and now look at you. Completely in your element, everything under control."

"I always knew you could do it," Cici agreed with an approving nod. "It's just a matter of making up your mind to get things done."

Paul and Derrick glanced at each other, and then smiled. "So it is," Paul agreed.

Bridget closed the refrigerator door, a bowlful of fresh eggs in her hands. "We're going to have you boys over for dinner before Christmas," she said, "so save an evening for us."

"And of course you'll all be our guests for Sunday brunch," Derrick returned generously. "Bring the family."

There were more hugs and good-byes, and when the men reached their car they sat there for a moment, shoulders slumped, thinking.

"The tree trimming party idea was brilliant," Paul offered in a moment. "So was Farley."

"Too bad neither of them worked."

Paul sighed. "I'm afraid I wasn't much help. I was just so embarrassed to be asking for help again. Particularly after we'd been doing so well on our own the last few months."

"And they are so beastly efficient," agreed Derrick.

"Which is precisely why they could have whipped everything into shape at the Hummingbird House in an afternoon."

"And it's not as though we wouldn't have done the same for them."

"Except they never would have asked us to."

"Right." It was Derrick's turn to sigh. "Well, we certainly can't ask them now. We're on our own. On the other hand," he added, with an obvious effort to look on the bright side, "we did at least have the foresight not to take any reservations between now and Christmas. Our schedule is clear."

Paul did not look cheered. "I suppose we could put an ad in the paper," he said in a moment.

"Too late for that. It wouldn't even come out until next week."

Paul looked at Derrick solemnly. "We should have spent less time in the planning stage."

Derrick nodded agreement and they sat there for a time, considering. Then, with a silent nod of resignation, Paul started the engine. "Well," he said, "let's go talk to Purline about cutting down some trees."

FIVE

The Plum Room

Angela Phipps walked into her husband's study just in time to see him slip what was clearly a small wrapped present into his desk drawer and turn the key in the lock. It was probably some overdone piece of jewelry or another, which he knew perfectly well would go straight from its box to the safe at the bank without her ever even trying it on. His gifts were really little more than investments these days, and had been for years. Which was why she was so puzzled—and frankly, annoyed—by the Christmas card he had left on her dressing table, with the brochure and reservation confirmation inside.

"What is this?" she demanded, dropping the brochure on the table.

He slipped the desk key into his pocket as he turned, smiling that automatic smile of his that had become his signature over the years, the one that never, ever reached his eyes. "Why, my love, it's just my way of saying Merry Christmas. I thought you might enjoy a little getaway in the mountains this holiday."

"Oh, for God's sake." Her tone was a cross

between exasperation and disgust. "A getaway in the mountains is a weekend at Sun Mountain or Telluride. The last thing I have time for is a trip across country to some backwoods lodge in the Shenandoah Valley. What in the world were you thinking?"

"I was thinking," he replied evenly, and the smile never wavered, "that we both could do with an escape from the holiday madness. Some time to relax and contemplate."

She looked at him sharply. "Contemplate what?"

"Maybe," he replied, still smiling that cold, dead smile of his, "what it was we used to like about each other."

Angela drew in a sharp breath for a reply, and released it unspoken. They faced each other across the desk, and across a wall of tension so thick it seemed to dim the light in the room. "Why?" she said at last.

Angela and Bryce Phipps lived in a two-story condo in one of the most prestigious buildings in Seattle, complete with views of the water and the Space Needle. The interior was tastefully decorated with collectibles from trips they had taken to Africa, India and China, although they had not actually taken any of those trips together. Their dinner parties were elegant and sophisticated, and invitations to them were highly sought after. In public they were a warm and charming couple, schooled in the art of conversation and in making others feel important. In private, they rarely spoke at all. It wasn't that there was any particular unresolved animosity between them. It was simply that they had nothing to say.

Bryce actually seemed to consider her question. "I'm not sure, really," he said in a moment. Then he shrugged. "Perhaps you're right. I don't know what I was thinking. I'll cancel."

Angela turned to leave, satisfied, but paused when the photograph on the brochure caught her eye. It was of a rustic-looking lodge in the snow at twilight. Golden light shone from the windows, and along the long front porch was a series of quirky-looking doors, each one painted a different color. While the snow was clearly Photoshopped, something about the light in the windows, those peculiar painted doors, reminded her of Christmases from her childhood. Her father had been mad for Christmas, and always found a way to make each one more fun, more exciting and filled with playful adventure, than the last. Looking at the picture of the lodge in the snow, she suddenly missed him intensely.

It has been said that a woman with a good father will marry a good man. Angela Phipps had married a good man, and she had proceeded to destroy him. Would it be such a terrible thing to accept his gesture at face value, just once? After all, it might be the last one he made.

She released a soft breath and spun the brochure

around toward him with the tip of one exquisitely manicured finger. "Oh for heaven's sake," she said. "I suppose I can bear one weekend in the woods. Of course, it will mean canceling the theater on the twenty-third, and the hospital dinner on the twenty-second, and I'm not at all sure what kind of message it will send to the Disadvantaged Children's Fundraising Committee when their chairperson doesn't show up for their gala event, but if this is what you're set on doing for the holidays . . ."

He said, "I am, actually." He wasn't smiling any longer. He just looked tired.

"Well then," she said. "I suppose I'd better start making phone calls. And Bryce . . ." Suddenly she felt as tired as he looked. Tired of pretending, tired of trying, tired of going on. "No gifts. Whatever you've locked in your drawer, take it back. I don't want it."

When she was gone, Bryce sat down heavily in his chair and, after a moment, unlocked the desk drawer. He looked at the wrapped box inside, but did not take it out. "Oh, my dear," he said softly, "I think you do."

SIX

O Christmas Tree

As it turned out, cutting down one's own Christmas tree was not nearly as challenging a task as Paul and Derrick had expected, particularly when they discovered they didn't actually have to handle any sharp implements—or, perhaps more importantly, scuff their suede Mark McNairy boots by trudging all over the mountainside searching out the perfect tree. The Christmas tree farm to which Purline directed them actually had golf carts with a driver assigned to each one. All they had to do was ride in the back while the vehicle cruised up and down the rows of spruce and fir, directing it to stop when they spied a likely candidate. They then got out, examined the prospect from proverbial head to toe, and declared Yay or Nay. If Yay, the driver got out, felled the tree with his trusty chain saw, and tagged it with their purchase number. It was, all in all, a most pleasant way to spend a crisp December afternoon.

They chose a fourteen-foot Douglas fir for the reception parlor, two ten-foot spruces for the dining porch, and a four-foot white pine for each of the seven guest rooms. After some debate, they

71

decided the entrance door could be much improved by a live tree on either side of it, decorated with velvet ribbon and their collection of white candle lights, so they bought two more eight-foot spruces. Ladybug Farm didn't have anything that grand.

"It's really quite satisfying, isn't it?" Derrick said as they stood in line to pay for their purchases. "Going out into the wild to claim and cut your own tree. I never understood before why the whole thing has been so romanticized, but now I see the appeal."

"It rather puts me in mind of the whole safari concept, which I never understood either," mused Paul, "despite how Jeff and Doug are always going on and on about man against nature and the majesty of the beast. Although," he added quickly, "this is a good deal more sustainable."

"I should certainly say," agreed Derrick. Before allowing saw blade to touch the first tree, they had demanded assurances from the driver that yes, as the announcement at the welcome station stated, it was the policy of this farm to plant two trees for every one that was cut. "And certainly more fulfilling to play the role of lumberjack than that of great white hunter."

Paul nodded enthusiastic agreement and warmed his hands inside the pockets of his fur-lined zippered vest. The line moved forward.

"You know," Derrick said, "the problem really

isn't getting all the decorating done before the first guest arrives. The problem is getting it all done before Sunday brunch. I mean, a late start can be overlooked up to this point, but this will be our last public brunch before Christmas, and we have a dozen reservations already. People will be expecting festivity."

"Well," Paul allowed, "it's our first year. The important thing was to get all of the arrangements in place for Christmas weekend. Next year we'll start earlier."

Derrick lifted his eyebrows. "Earlier than August?"

"Not to worry," Paul replied with a wave of his leather-gloved hand. "It's not as though neither of us has ever decorated a Christmas tree before."

"I worked my way through college as an assistant window dresser at Macy's during the holidays," Derrick reminded him heartily, just as he had done eight or nine times a year for the past thirty Christmases.

"And at least the wreaths are all done," Paul said. "All we really have left are the mantelscapes and the trees."

"And the outdoor decor," Derrick added, "including lights, which *really* should be done by a professional. And the tablescapes for the dining room and the tea table, and weren't we going to put moss topiaries in the powder rooms?"

"All prepared and waiting in the storage room,"

Paul assured him. "All we have to do is make the lace roses and hot glue on the peppermint-candy ornaments."

"It certainly seems like a lot," Derrick worried.

"For what our guests are paying," Paul replied, "they deserve a lot."

The man in front of them finished paying and moved on, and Paul and Derrick stepped up to the window.

The booth was little more than a plywood shack painted, rather badly, with a row of evergreens on each side. A fresh-faced youth in a red Santa hat greeted them. "Merry Christmas, gentlemen. May I see your ticket please?"

"And a very merry Christmas to you, too, my good man," Paul replied warmly, handing him the yellow slip with their purchases recorded on it. "I was told our order would be awaiting us at the gate?"

"Yes, sir, it's on its way." He started adding up the purchases on an old-fashioned adding machine. "Quite a few trees you got there. You decorating a church?"

Paul smiled and produced a card from his pocket. "The Hummingbird House Bed and Breakfast. Fine accommodations for discerning guests, brunch every Sunday from ten until two. Tell your friends."

The young man took the card and glanced at it. "Because we give a discount for churches."

"We're not a church," Paul told him.

"Although we go to church," Derrick hastened to add. Then, looking uncomfortable, "As often as we can, anyway. What I mean is, with the brunch on Sundays it's rather difficult . . ."

"He's not interested, Derrick," murmured Paul, and took out his wallet. "The total?"

"We offer a discount for clergy," Derrick said, perhaps a little too adamantly.

Paul lifted an eyebrow at him and Derrick insisted, "We do."

The clerk waited to make sure he was finished, then turned to Paul. "That'll be two hundred forty dollars. Is that Visa or MasterCard?"

"What a bargain," Derrick murmured as Paul handed over his MasterCard. "We spent more than that on our foyer tree at home."

"But," Paul reminded him, "it came fully decorated."

"True," agreed Derrick.

The clerk returned Paul's card just as a big tractor hauling a wagon filled with evergreens chugged into view. "That must be your order now, sir," said the young man, smiling. "Just pull your vehicle up to the gate and I'll call a couple of men to help you load. Did you bring a truck or a trailer?"

Paul looked at Derrick, who stared back at him. They both stared at the clerk. "Wait," Paul said. "Do you mean you don't deliver?"

• • •

After only an hour or so of panic, Harmony was able to pull off one last Christmas miracle before she left for the mysteries of the Far East. One of her event vendors had a truck he used to deliver rental furniture and a driver available. Both arrived bright and early the following morning, and before noon their Christmas trees were unloaded into the drive of the Hummingbird House. It cost them a hundred dollars, plus gas, mileage and tip for the driver, but neither of them complained.

"Harmony, you are a lifesaver!" Derrick declared as they watched the delivery truck drive away. "Whatever are we going to do without you?"

They stood on the front porch gazing out with relief over the mountain of evergreen trees in their driveway, Harmony in an outrageous floor-length faux leopard fur coat, and the men in their country-casual heavy wool sweaters. Harmony's luggage was piled around her—quite a bit more than one might necessarily imagine needing at a minimalist ashram retreat—as she waited for her driver to arrive to take her to the airport. She beamed her thanks and patted Derrick's cheek with a gloved hand. "Darling, I'll be back before you know it."

"And don't forget you've still got to get all them trees in the house," Purline pointed out sourly, rubbing her arms against the cold. She, too, had come out onto the porch to watch the unloading, but did not appear to be nearly as thrilled about it as the other three were. "And don't take all day about doing it, either, because I've got to go behind you and sweep up the pine needles. And what're you expectin' to do about stands?"

Alarm flashed across the two men's eyes, but Harmony gave a light dismissing laugh. "They arrived yesterday with the poinsettias and greenery. Just look in the box marked 'tree stands.' They're completely adjustable, you'll have no trouble at all."

Purline muttered, "Sez you." She went back inside, letting the screen door slam firmly as she did.

Paul turned to Harmony. "My dear," he said sincerely, "I know we don't always see eye-to-eye, but you have truly risen to the occasion this time."

"Only one of many," Derrick pointed out quickly.

"Agreed," Paul admitted. "And even though you are leaving us in somewhat of a lurch . . ."

"Although I'm sure the two massage therapists you've arranged will be fabulous," Derrick put in, only a little anxiously. "They're arriving Wednesday, right?"

Paul went on, "I can't think of a better time than this moment to present you with this tiny holiday token of our good regards." He reached into his pocket and brought out a small flat box wrapped in silver foil and elegantly tied with a fuchsia ribbon. "Merry Christmas, Harmony."

"They're earrings," Derrick blurted excitedly. "Hand-hammered by a Navajo princess from silver artisanally mined in Arizona and infused with the spirit of the wolf." And at Paul's small eyeroll, he added defensively, "That's what it said on the card."

"Oh, boys." Harmony's overly made-up face lit up with the gentle light of a church luminary as she took the box from Paul. "I don't know what to say."

"Feel free to add feathers and beads," said Paul, who made no secret of his dismay over Harmony's taste in jewelry. But he smiled when he said it, and Harmony threw her arms around his neck and hugged him hard, then did the same to Derrick.

"You two are just so . . . surprising!" she declared as she stepped away, beaming. Her rather bulbous nose was red and she wiped a tiny speck of moisture from her eyes. Derrick surreptitiously did the same.

"Of course," she added cheerfully, "I don't participate in the pagan ritual of holiday gift exchange, which has really become a hopeless pawn of corporate America, but as it happens I've arranged a little surprise for you boys, too. Oh!

There's my car. Help me with these bags, will you, darlings?"

They loaded her small mountain of luggage into the Town Car, and in a flurry of blown kisses and leopard fur, Harmony was gone. Paul and Derrick stood on the steps, looking bemused and more than a little uneasy. "A surprise from Harmony," murmured Paul. "Why do I think that can't be a good thing?"

"Oh, it could be quite good," Derrick assured him. "It could be a thirty-foot yacht or a resort hotel in Sri Lanka. But," he admitted, "it probably isn't."

"Right," agreed Paul.

Gazing once again over the pile of Christmas greenery in their driveway, the two heaved a collective sigh. "How much," inquired Derrick dolefully, "do you suspect it weighs?"

"In total?" Paul's expression was speculative. "Well over a ton, I would guess."

Derrick spread out his fingers. "These hands," he said, "were never meant for manual labor."

Paul shot him an indignant look. "Like mine were?"

"And I haven't wanted to mention it, but my back has been bothering me lately."

"Oh, please."

Derrick gathered his resolve. "Of course, I really should have clearance from my cardiologist before undertaking any strenuous physical activity."

Paul glared at him. "Seriously? You're playing the heart card?"

"It would appear," replied Derrick evenly, "that's the only card I have left."

For a moment they were at a standoff, and then Paul decided grumpily, "Well, they sat outside all night, I don't suppose it will hurt them to stay in the yard a little while longer. Besides, we have to assemble the stands first. We'll make an action plan after lunch."

"Assembling stands," declared Derrick happily, "now *that* sounds like a task worthy of my talents. Fashioning lace roses, making bows for the garland, designing table decor . . . those are the kinds of things I'm suited for. The importance of doing the work you're meant to do simply cannot be overstated."

"Now all we have to do is find someone who was meant to do manual labor."

"I'll get the stands," Derrick said.

Paul said, "I'll get the toolbox."

To which Derrick replied, "We have a toolbox?"

Paul ignored him and went around the porch toward the toolshed while Derrick went into the house. He cut through the kitchen, which was filled with the delectable aromas of soup simmering on the stove and something sweet and fruity baking in the oven. He stopped to lift the lid from what appeared to be a vegetable soup with wild rice and mushrooms, inhaling the fragrance appreciatively, and then he pushed through the swinging door of the butler's pantry on his way to the storage room that lay beyond. There he stopped.

Every piece of silver they owned was scattered across the trestle worktable, platters, urns, bowls, serving pieces, dinnerware, vases. And in the center of it all was a dark-haired, doe-eyed, nut-brown girl in a red calico dress, one of the silver candlesticks Derrick had gotten in Prague clutched in each of her fists. She let out a startled squeal when she saw him and Derrick let out a gasp. He backed out the swinging door and into the kitchen, crying, "Purline!" Just as Paul burst in from the outside, calling, "Purline!" and looking as distracted as Derrick was.

Derrick pointed helplessly to the pantry. "There's an urchin in there with all our silver!"

"There are children in the toolshed!" Paul cried just as Purline raced into the kitchen, a dustcloth in one hand and a can of spray polish in the other.

"What?" she demanded, breathing hard. "Who screamed? What's wrong?"

With his arm still lifted toward the pantry, Derrick began, "Purline, there's a . . ."

Paul interrupted, "Purline, did you know there were two . . ."

Understanding dawned as they each came to the same conclusion.

"Your children," Derrick said. They had been so

preoccupied with the Christmas trees that neither of them had noticed when Purline came to work, and of course they had far too much on their minds to remember the children she had told them she was bringing today.

At that moment, the door to the pantry swung open and the little girl came out, still clutching one of the candlesticks. Purline put aside the cleaning supplies and opened her arms to the child, her face breaking into a tender smile. "Mimi, come here to Mommy."

Mimi complied, her expression solemn, and Purline stood the child in front of her, stroking her hair affectionately. "Sweetpea, this is Mr. Paul and Mr. Derrick. They're mommy's bosses, or at least they think they are. This is my little girl Naomi," she told the two men. "Mimi for short. She's eight years old." She looked down at her daughter. "Say hello, and then get back to work."

"Hello, Mr. Paul and Mr. Derrick," she said in a voice so sweet and earnest that even Paul's lips quirked with amusement. "I'm sorry I screamed at you, Mr. Derrick."

Purline gave a brusque, approving nod, her lips tightening with an almost repressed smile. "She's smart as a whip. I know she don't look that much like me, but that's because she's adopted. We brought her back from a mission trip to Honduras when she was six years old."

"Ah," exclaimed Paul. "That explains it."

"We wondered how you could have school-age children when you're so young," Derrick explained.

She said pertly, "Well, now you know. Or you could've just asked."

"Well, it hardly seemed appropriate," Paul demurred.

Derrick said helpfully, "We talked about adopting when we were younger."

"But since neither of us actually like children . . ." Paul let the sentence trail off with a self-explanatory shrug.

"We tabled the idea," Derrick concluded.

The back door opened and two small, brown-haired, freckle-faced boys in matching red parkas came in on a gust of cold air, surveying the two men suspiciously. No one could doubt that these two belonged to anyone but Purline.

"These here are the twins," Purline said, "Jacob and Joshua. They started kindergarten this year. Boys, this is Mr. Paul and Mr. Derrick."

"Well, now," said Paul, clearly feigning enthusiasm, "fine-looking young men, I'm sure. But, Purline, I'm afraid we really can't have them playing in the toolshed. There are far too many dangerous things in there."

Purline looked skeptical. "How would you know? The last time you were anywhere near the toolshed was to unlock it for the yard man."

"And I'm afraid that goes for the silverware,

too," Derrick said, ignoring her. He took a hesitant step forward, smiling apologetically at the little girl, and snatched the candlestick from her hand. "I'm sorry, my dear, but some of these pieces are quite valuable. Surely you can find a nice coloring book instead?"

Purline gave him an exasperated look and took the candlestick. "She's not playing with it, she's *polishing* it. Didn't you say all that silver had to be done by Friday?"

"Well, yes, but . . ."

"Mr. Derrick," put in young Naomi earnestly. "What is valuable?"

Derrick put on his kindest smile as he bent down to her. "It means worth a lot of money."

"Or it can mean 'treasured,'" added Paul.

"In whichever case," said Derrick, "it means you must take very good care of it because it's not a toy."

"We need a lot of money," said one of the twins behind him.

Both Paul and Derrick looked at him, concerned. "You do?"

The two boys nodded gravely. "We have to buy a goat."

"A goat?"

Naomi explained, "To send to Africa."

"So the children can go to school," added one of the twins.

"And have shoes," said the other.

Paul looked at Purline helplessly, "I'm afraid I'm lost. You're sending a goat to Africa?"

"It's their Christmas project for Sunday School," she explained. "You know, the goat makes milk, the milk makes cheese, they sell the cheese, the goat has babies, they sell the babies, the babies have babies and pretty soon everybody in town is making cheese and buying shoes and going to school."

"Oh!" exclaimed Derrick, enlightened. "Well, we'll be glad to contribute, of course. How much do you need?"

She gave him a quelling look. "Get your own goat. This is for the kids."

"But," Paul put in, "surely a little help . . ."

"The Lord helps those who help themselves," she interrupted firmly, and turned to the boys. "Did you find the rake in the shed where I said it was?"

The two of them nodded, in unison, and replied, in unison, "Yes, ma'am."

"Then get out there and start raking out the flower beds like I showed you. When you get a nice big pile, you come on in and I'll make you a grilled cheese."

"Yes, ma'am!"

The twins raced out, slamming the door behind them. Purline returned the candlestick to the little girl and gave her a pat on the bottom. "Go on, scoot. We both've got to get ourselves back to work."

"Purline," said Paul, alarmed, "we really can't ask your children to work for us."

"You don't have to," returned Purline. "I am."

"But," objected Derrick, "there are child labor laws!"

"It's their holiday!" added Paul. "Surely they could just sit quietly and . . . and watch television or something?"

She scowled at them. "Idle hands are the devil's workshop, everybody knows that, and I'm raising good Christian children. You think I'm gonna go to all the trouble to feed them and put clothes on their backs and nurse them when they're sick and carry them back and forth to school every day for eighteen years just to see them end up in federal prison? No sirree, you can bet I won't! My kids are going to learn the value of a dollar just like I had to when I was their age. Besides," she added, picking up her dustcloth again, "how else are they gonna earn money for that goat? I'm paying them a nickel an hour. Lunch'll be ready in half an hour."

With that, she sashayed out of the kitchen, swinging the door in her wake, and there wasn't much left for Paul or Derrick to say.

In a moment Derrick ventured, "They seem nice enough."

"As far as children go," agreed Paul.

"But they'll never earn enough money for a goat before Christmas," Derrick said.

"Not at a nickel an hour."

"I understand the concept of working for a reward, I do. It's rather sweet, really. But . . ."

"Perhaps we could offer to increase their salary," Paul suggested.

"You'll do no such thing!" Purline called from beyond the swinging door, and Paul and Derrick both winced guiltily.

She pushed back through the door, hands on her hips, glaring at them. "They're my kids and I'll raise them the way I see fit. Don't y'all have some trees to put up? Do I have to chase you out of here with a broom?"

"But Purline . . ."

She shifted her eyes around the kitchen. "Where's my broom?"

Paul raised a hand in self-defense. "What I was going to say," he persisted, "is that it looks as though we're going to require some additional assistance with the trees."

"All of the decorating really," Derrick put in, "if we expect to have it done before Sunday."

"Do you know anyone who might be able to help?" asked Paul.

A corner of her lips turned down sourly. "That's what you get for leaving everything till the last minute, and depending on that crazy woman to get it done. And no, I don't know anybody that's got time to help. Besides, the Lord . . ."

"Helps those who help themselves," Derrick finished with a sigh. "Yes, we know."

"I don't even know what that means," Paul grumbled.

"It means you'd better get busy," retorted Purline. She turned smartly on her heel to leave and then stopped, head cocked toward the window. "Y'all expecting company?"

It took them a moment to realize that the low rumbling that grew louder with every moment was the sound of a motorcycle engine, and even when they went to the window and saw it for themselves they could hardly believe it. The big black beast skirted the mountain of Christmas trees in the drive and made its way to the back parking lot, powerful engine chugging and pulsing. There it stopped, and the rider got off. By this time there were three faces crowded at the kitchen window, their breath making individual circles on the pane.

"I wasn't expecting anyone, were you?" Paul said.

"He certainly doesn't look familiar," Derrick replied.

He was a big man in jeans and boots with chains, wearing a black leather jacket and blue bandanna skull cap, beneath which a long pony-tail trailed down his back. Tattoos were visible on his hands and neck. He approached the porch of the Hummingbird House with a swaggering, confident stride.

"Looks like he's up to no good to me," Purline observed suspiciously.

"Patrons of the Hummingbird House don't ride motorcycles," agreed Derrick. He thought about that for a moment. "At least they haven't so far."

Paul pushed away from the window and started toward the back door. "Well, we can't just stand here staring at him. We're in the hospitality business, after all."

"You be careful," Purline urged, following close behind. "My kids're out there."

Paul gave her an uncertain look, and then opened the door.

"Good morning, sir!" he called out, perhaps a trifle too heartily. "How are you this fine morning?"

Thus encouraged, the stranger took the steps two at a time, his hand extended. "Top of the world, my brother," he replied in a distinctive Australian accent. "And yourself?"

He was an interesting-looking fellow. He had bright blue eyes, mutton chops down to his chin, and a nose that appeared to have been broken more than once. But his smile was good and his grip solid. It was, in fact, perhaps a little too solid, and Paul had to flex his fingers when they were released.

Paul said, "I'm Paul Slater, and this is . . ." He glanced behind him for his partner, who reluctantly came forward. "Derrick Anderson. We're the proprietors of the Hummingbird House. Do you have a reservation, by chance?"

"I do not," admitted the stranger. "What I do have is a strong back and a willing pair of hands. And while I see you're fully staffed in the lawn maintenance department . . ." He glanced with a twinkling eye toward the twins, who stood staring with the rake clutched between them. "I wonder if you might have need for a helping hand here and there about the place, it being the holiday season and all."

Paul drew a delighted breath to reply but was stopped by a hard tug on the hem of his sweater. He glanced back to meet Purline's white-eyed gaze, motioning him back inside the house with an exaggerated jerk of her chin. He returned an uneasy smile to the stranger and said, "Just one moment, please."

He stepped back into the kitchen without completely closing the door, and Purline hissed, "Are you crazy? You're not going to take a complete stranger in this house without knowing a thing about him!"

"Actually," Derrick pointed out a little timidly, "that's kind of what we do."

"Nobody just rides up to a house and asks for work," Purline went on, ignoring Derrick, "not in this day and age. He's probably staking out the place right this minute. He could be a serial killer or worse!"

"What's worse than a serial killer?" Paul said.

"He's not even from around here," Purline said.

"Just ask him if he's got references. Just ask him."

"We didn't ask you for references," Paul pointed out.

She scowled. "That's different."

"How?"

"Because if you'd've asked, I would've had them!"

"And come to think of it," Paul added, "*you* just walked in one day and asked for work."

Her scowl grew fiercer. "Now you listen here to me . . ."

"Oh my goodness," Derrick said softly. Sudden, delighted understanding dawned in his eyes. "Harmony!"

Purline broke off and both she and Paul turned to Derrick, looking confused. Then Paul's face broke into a delighted smile. "Harmony's surprise!"

Paul turned to Purline and gave her arm a reassuring pat. "Not to worry, my dear. He has references. Harmony sent him!"

Purline did not look in the least reassured as Paul and Derrick went back out onto the porch.

"Mister, um . . ." Paul faltered, and the stranger stepped forward, smiling.

"Michael," he said. "Call me Mick."

"Wonderful," Paul said, rubbing his hands together in satisfaction. "Mr. Michaels, we're delighted you're here."

"Delighted," parroted Derrick, although he couldn't help looking at the traces of ink that peeked from beneath the wrists of the leather jacket.

"We find ourselves a bit behind with our holiday chores," Paul went on, "and the truth is . . ." He glanced at Derrick. "Well, our talents really don't lie in the area of manual labor."

"Fortunately," replied Mick cheerfully, "mine do. And I think it's very important for everyone to do what they're suited for."

Derrick brightened. "I was saying that only a moment ago! You are a godsend, Mr. Michaels!" He grabbed the other man's hand and pumped it enthusiastically.

"Please," replied the stranger, smiling, "it's Mick."

"All right then." Derrick stepped back, beaming. "Mick, welcome to the Hummingbird House." Then, "What do you know about hanging Christmas lights?"

"Whatever you need me to," Mick assured him, and Paul and Derrick exchanged a triumphant look.

"Welcome aboard, Mick," Paul declared, opening the door wide for him. "Come in, we'll show you around and talk about what we had in mind. Have you had lunch? No? Purline, set another plate."

Purline glared at him, and Paul could not help returning a smirk as he edged past her on his way to join Derrick and Mick for the tour. "What do you know about that, Purline?" he said. "You were right. The Lord *does* help those who help themselves."

He quickened his step and called ahead, "If you're ready to start right after lunch, the first thing we could use your help with is situating a few Christmas trees."

"All in all," declared Paul as he poured them each a glass of after-dinner sherry that evening, "a most satisfying day. I'll admit, I was a bit uncertain when it started out, but in the end . . . voila." He gestured with one of the glasses to the Christmas tree, complete with lights, silver and blue ribbons, and hundreds of sparkling glass hummingbirds, that graced the parlor. Since Derrick was not actually in the room as he spoke, he put the other glass on the small table beside the fireplace and stepped back to once again admire the Christmas tree.

Of course, that was the only tree in the house that was completely decorated. But all of the stands had been assembled and filled with the proper sized tree, the garland had been draped around the windows and doors, and all of the wreaths had been hung. While placing the hooks for the outdoor lighting, Mick had discovered a sagging gutter, which he promised to replace the following day. Work would then begin on the light display for the garden, and Mick had every confidence that the delicate hummingbird light sculpture, whose wings were designed to flutter every time it dipped its head to drink from the fountain, would be fully operational by Sunday. Paul found himself hoping for a dark and gloomy Sunday so that the brunch guests could enjoy the show.

Derrick came into the room, the telephone handset in his hand, a puzzled look on his face. "The most peculiar thing," he said.

Paul, still gazing at the tree proudly, replied, "Magnificent, isn't it? Exactly what I pictured when we bought the place."

"I just got off the phone with Harmony," Derrick said, and Paul looked at him. "I wanted to thank her for sending Mick, and I managed to catch her on her layover in London. She didn't know what I was talking about. She didn't send him."

Paul was silent, letting the news sink in. "I don't know which is more alarming," he said in a moment. "The possibility that Purline was right about Mick, or the thought that there is still a surprise from Harmony somewhere in our future."

Derrick nodded glum agreement. Then he cheered marginally. "Maybe he won't come back."

Paul said, "Maybe." But he did not look happy about it.

When the fading daylight put an end to the

workday, Mick had roared off on his motorcycle with a promise to return bright and early the next morning. Paul had wanted to pay him cash for the day's work, but he insisted he wouldn't accept payment until the job was finished, which seemed to Paul the mark of an honest man. Surely the mark of a criminal would have been to take the money and *then* run. Wouldn't it?

Then Derrick brightened. "It was probably the girls. They heard he was looking for work and sent him over."

Paul suggested, "We could call and ask."

Derrick hesitated. "He really can do anything, you know. Do you remember that outlet that was malfunctioning on the back porch? He rewired it there on the spot."

"He's a steady worker, and fast. He got every one of those trees set up and the garland hung without taking a break."

"And he said he'd trim back that poplar branch that's been obscuring our view all summer," Derrick said. "You know how hard we've tried to get someone out to do that."

Paul lifted an eyebrow. "Did he?" He took a sip of his sherry. "You know, it really was a small miracle, the way everything turned out."

"And you don't question miracles," Derrick said.

"Purline would say we should count our blessings."

"Besides," added Derrick, "the girls probably sent him."

"I'm sure of it," agreed Paul.

Derrick picked up his sherry and took his chair beside the fireplace. Paul settled into the chair opposite and they sat in contented silence, admiring the tree and counting their blessings.

SEVEN

The Magnolia Suite

Outside the elegantly appointed master retreat, Carl Bartlett could hear what he had come to think of as the usual clatter and dissonance of family life: petulant voices raised in anger, the thumping bass notes of rap music played too loud, the crash and slam of objects both breakable and unbreakable. His wife's voice, sometimes strident, sometimes pleading, sometimes completely out of patience. The retorts of his two teenage daughters: sharp, disrespectful, dismissive. Everyone lived like this. Didn't they?

When he was at home, which was not very often, Carl kept the door closed to whatever room he was in, hoping, like a cowardly ostrich with his head in the sand, that if he stayed hidden long enough the storm would pass him by. It would not, of course. He knew that now. The storm, it seemed, was of his own making, and it would follow him for the rest of his life no matter where he went.

He wasn't sure how everything had gotten so out of hand. It would have been different if he had been a bad man, a cruel father or an indifferent husband. But he loved his wife. He loved his daughters. Everything he had ever done, or ever would do, was for them. Everything.

He went to the window, pushed back the ivory satin drape, and stood for a moment looking out at the Christmas lights that twinkled throughout the neighborhood. They lived in a big brick house overlooking the river, in a gated community where the lots were large, the houses set far apart, and the taste level of outdoor Christmas decorations was strictly regulated. The tacky lawn snowmen and high-wattage roof lights of Carl's childhood had no place here. He missed that.

The girls were just outside the bedroom door now; they must know he could hear them. Perhaps that was the point.

"This is the lamest thing *ever,* Mom!" That was Kelly, the youngest. She had a nose ring. How that had happened Carl hadn't a clue. "Disney World? Are you kidding me? I'm fourteen, for God's sake!"

"Jason's mom said it was okay if I spent the holidays with them." That was Pam, his sixteen-year-old. She had a spider tattoo behind her left ear. "All the way to New Year's! You don't believe me, just call her up!"

"Stop it, both of you!" Carl's wife, Leona, sounded close to the edge, her voice at that register that was just below screaming. "This is the first time your father has had two weeks off in fifteen years, and we're going on a family vacation, do you hear me? I don't want another word about it!"

"But why does he have to ruin Christmas? I have plans!"

"Two weeks!" Kelly cried. "I'll die!"

"Why doesn't he just go back to work?" Pam added spitefully. "Everybody's happier when he's not here anyway."

That hurt, Carl would not deny it. But he had discovered over the past several years that when the pain inside you was so big you couldn't remember a time when it wasn't there, those little pinpricks weren't quite as noticeable as they once might have been.

He went to his dresser and opened the top drawer. From beneath a neatly folded stack of sweaters he withdrew a manila envelope and opened it. He pulled out the top sheet of the stack of papers inside, the one addressed to the Attorney General of the State of Virginia.

Sir, it read, *pursuant to our conversation of December 1, I enclose the following documents . . .*

That was as far as he got before he heard the doorknob turn. It occurred to him that Leona might have deliberately chosen to finish the fight with the girls outside the bedroom door so that he could hear it. Perhaps she expected him to intervene. Perhaps she wanted him to sympathize with what she had to put up with everyday.

Perhaps she just wanted to punish him. It didn't matter. None of it did.

He slipped the letter back into the envelope. It was only a copy, as were the pages that accompanied it. The originals had been mailed yesterday. It was done. There was no turning back now.

"Go to your rooms," Leona said sharply, "and finish packing. We're going to be on the road by seven in the morning."

"I won't even be awake at seven in the morning!"

"I'm not going! I'll run away!"

With the door open a crack, Carl could hear every word clearly.

"You're going, damn it! We're all going! We're going and you're going to pretend to have a good time whether you like it or not! Get used to it!"

Carl returned the envelope to its hiding place beneath the stack of sweaters just as Leona came into the room, slamming the door behind her. "Sometimes I wish she *would* run away, the ungrateful little . . ." She stopped herself with a breath and leaned against the door tiredly. She grimaced as Carl turned away from the dresser, one of the sweaters in his hand. "The very thought of two weeks in a car with those two is making me break out in hives. God give me strength."

Carl walked to the bed and put the sweater in the suitcase that was open there. Leona pushed away from the door and added quickly, "Not that

I don't think it's a wonderful idea, darling, all of us going away for the holidays together, and you were so sweet to think of it, but the girls *are* a little old for Disney World, and God, a whole week with your mother? And I've got to be honest, that lodge in the woods? What on earth is there for them to do there?"

She walked over to the inlaid walnut dressing table in the sitting alcove and poured herself a measure of bourbon from the decanter atop it. She liked to think if she kept the booze in her bedroom the girls wouldn't know how much she drank. They did.

Carl said, turning away from the suitcase, "We had such a good time at Disney World when we took the girls the last time. And Mother's house is only twenty minutes away. She hasn't seen the kids in three years."

Leona gestured to him in a questioning manner with the decanter. He shook his head and she started to replace the cap, then changed her mind and poured another splash into her glass. "Darling, the last time we took a trip together was ten years ago, and there's a huge difference between the ages of six and sixteen when it comes to children. And now Jason's folks have invited Pammie on this ski trip next week, and my life will be absolute hell for the rest of the school year if she doesn't get to go. Not to mention Kelly, who's had her dress picked out for Amy Brenton's party for six months and . . ." She interrupted herself to take a sturdy drink from her glass, then dropped down to the club chair beside the window and crossed her long legs with a sigh. "Sweetheart, I know you mean well, but honestly, I can't think what's gotten into you. You don't even know these kids." She said it without accusation or rancor, merely stating a fact. "Why on earth would you want to spend two weeks with them?"

He turned to look at her. She was as beautiful as the day he had married her, with gleaming dark hair falling in graceful waves over her shoulders, a flawless complexion, perfect smile and a size-four figure that was meant for wearing the latest fashions from Paris or New York. She was, in short, everything his money could buy, and she worked hard at staying that way. If he met her today he would fall in love with her all over again.

He, by contrast, had aged considerably. There were puffy circles around his eyes and ten extra pounds around his waist from the fifteen-hour days he spent behind a desk. His hair was thinning and his shoulders were stooped, and if she met him for the first time today, she wouldn't give him a second glance. Did she love him? He thought so. But it didn't matter. Not now.

He said, "I just wanted us to have one nice old-fashioned Christmas together. I wanted the kids to be kids and the family to be together. One Christmas. That's all."

She sipped her drink, frowning a little. "Maybe if we gave her the car," she said.

"What?"

She made a vague circling gesture with her glass before taking another sip. "Pammie. She's been driving me out of my mind about a new MINI Cooper since Barb Singleton got one for her birthday. Maybe we should give it to her for Christmas."

He said, "Didn't we give her the Audi when she turned sixteen?"

"Well, yes, but it was a *family* car, not her own. Not a new car."

"It didn't even have five thousand miles on it," he objected.

She brightened and sipped from her glass. "Yes," she said. "A new car. That should do the trick. Now what about Kelly? How can we make this up to her?"

"Make it up to her? I'm giving them Disney World, a grandmother who'll spoil them silly, and a vacation package with sleigh rides and gourmet meals and spa treatments. What exactly am I supposed to be apologizing for?"

She looked exasperated. "Oh, Carl, honestly, haven't you been paying attention at all? What I'm trying to tell you is . . ." Her cell phone rang, and she dug it out of the pocket of her designer jeans, glancing at it in annoyance. "Damn, that's Susan Hiller. I promised to call her back three hours ago." She clicked on the phone and stood up, pasting a huge smile on her face. "Susan! Darling! I've been trying and trying to reach you, but your line has been busy. Now listen, I don't want you to worry one minute about the benefit ball. I have everything all worked out with Nigel, and he promised to e-mail you the list . . ." She walked out of the room, heels clicking on the hardwood floors, without glancing at Carl again.

Carl went back to his closet and took out the wrapped presents he had already bought for his wife and the girls. He tucked the gifts into his suitcase and hoped he would be forgiven the fact that none of the small boxes contained a new car.

He hoped he would be forgiven a lot of things.

EIGHT

Sunday Brunch

Sunday brunch at the Hummingbird House was an event that had become more or less legendary in the community, and even beyond. It wasn't so much the food (which, thanks to a combination of Paul's style, Derrick's obsession with Internet recipes, and Purline's cooking, was always tasty and beautifully presented) so much as it was the ambience and, in truth, the hosts themselves. Paul greeted each guest with a signature cocktail and a genuine delight in their company; Derrick could always be counted upon for the latest gossip as he wandered from table to table, making sure everyone was comfortable and well fed. Diners arrived early to sip their cocktails and peruse the art gallery that Derrick had created in the reception area, and lingered to while away the afternoon around the big stone fire pit that was set into one of the large patios, or lounge around the indoor fireplace, or wander through the gardens in season. Paul and Derrick didn't run a restaurant, they gave parties. And their guests came for more than a meal; they came to spend a pleasant Sunday with friends.

On this last brunch before Christmas, every

reservation was filled. Everyone wanted to see how the new owners of the Hummingbird House, who already had gained a reputation for going over the top with every venture, would decorate for the holidays and, thanks to Mick, they were not disappointed. Every bare-branched tree in the garden was glowing with miniature white lights and uplit with pink spotlights, so that, even on a moderately cloudy winter morning like this one, the effect was of a mystical garden at sunset. The day was a bit too bright to get the full effect of the hummingbird light sculpture, but the fountain was filled with silver Christmas balls that danced and twirled with the splash of water. The railings around the porch were draped with evergreen garland that was woven with tiny lights, and curtain lights cascaded from the eaves all around the lodge. Evergreen wreaths woven with silver and gold mesh and the appropriate color velvet ribbon decorated each of the painted exterior doors, and every window was encircled with greenery and twinkling lights. The guest rooms were still a work in progress, but the brunch guests ooh-ahhed over the hummingbird Christmas tree in the parlor, and admired the mantelscape of gold branches and oversized spheres in burgundy, emerald and sapphire satin studded with pearls and lace.

The seasonal cocktail of the day was an apple-cranberry martini served with complimentary toasted walnut cheese puffs. Two industrious-looking teenage waiters in red velvet vests and festive plaid bow ties served guests their choice of broccoli soup garnished with truffle oil or a winter salad with kale, blue cheese, dates and toasted pecans. For the entree there was a roast loin of pork with a cranberry-mustard reduction and buttermilk potatoes or herb roasted chicken with root vegetables, along with a variety of quiches and a lovely quinoa and lentil dish for the vegans. For dessert there was pumpkin cheesecake or tart cherry crepes with homemade vanilla ice cream.

Bridget came in with Lindsay and Cici a little before twelve, all of them dressed in their Sunday best and pink-cheeked with cold. The house, sparkling with holiday lights and redolent of good things from the kitchen, was already humming with voices and the tinkle of silver above an orchestral rendition of "Good King Wenceslas."

"Darlings, you look gorgeous!" Paul greeted them. He took their coats and kissed each chilly cheek. "Cocktails and nibbles in the parlor, come sit by the fire while I get your table ready." He glanced around. "Where is everyone else?"

Lindsay said, "Dominic's parking the car." She glanced at Cici, as though expecting her to speak, but she did not.

Paul prompted, "And the children?"

Cici made a small face. "They're at home."

"Packing," Bridget added with a sigh.

"Lori's dad surprised them with a two-week vacation to Cabo," Cici explained. "Kind of a combination wedding present and Christmas present."

"And who wouldn't want to go to Cabo this time of year?" Bridget put in, albeit somewhat wanly. "It was a lovely gesture. You know they never really had a honeymoon."

"And, with his typical thoughtlessness," Cici went on, "he sent the tickets yesterday for a flight that leaves in the morning. So the whole house has been in an uproar the past twenty-four hours trying to get them ready to go."

"But," Paul objected, "two weeks? That means they'll miss Christmas!"

Cici's mouth turned down bitterly and Bridget's eyes clouded. "Right," Cici said.

"However," Lindsay reminded them both, "we're not going to make them feel bad about it. They've both been through a lot this year and they really deserve this."

Bridget sighed again. "Right."

"Well, I don't think it's all right!" Paul declared indignantly. "Christmas won't be the same without Lori. That little scamp, I've a good mind to send her Christmas present right back to Neiman's!" Then he added charitably to Bridget, "But at least your daughter and grandchildren will be here."

She smiled. "You're right, and it's been ages

since I've seen them. But the point was to have the *whole* family together."

He patted her shoulder with one hand and Cici's with the other. "Now, now, my dears, come sit by the fire. I'll make your drinks extra strong."

He turned them toward the parlor where several couples sat sipping drinks, chatting and admiring the glittering Christmas tree. Cici exclaimed, "Oh, my, that's gorgeous! Where did you get all the hummingbirds?"

Paul beamed his pleasure. "Well, it was a challenge, I can assure you. But don't you love it?"

All three women assured him that they had never seen anything quite so beautiful, and then Lindsay added, sounding a little concerned, "Paul, who is that rough-looking guy we saw up on a ladder behind the garage?"

Paul's genial smile might have faltered just a fraction. "Oh, don't you know?" Then, rushing on, "That's Mick, the fellow responsible for all the splendor you see around you." He spread his arms expansively. "An absolute miracle worker, our good right arm, I simply don't know how we could have gotten through this past week without him. And . . ." He let the smile drop away as he looked from one to the other of them. "You didn't send him, did you?"

The women stared back at him. "Send him?" Cici said. "Why would we do that?"

"I thought," Paul began uncomfortably, "that is, we thought, when he showed up looking for work just hours after we mentioned we were looking for someone . . ."

Bridget's delicate eyebrows drew together in disapproval. "You hired him off the street?"

"Well, hardly off the street . . ."

"Someone you don't even know?" Lindsay put in.

"We can hardly know everyone," Paul objected.

"Oh, Paul." Cici's consternation was evident. "I really don't think you should have done that. You have to be so careful these days. I mean, what do you know about him?"

Paul went to the primitive pine sideboard beneath the window with its extravagant vase of holly, evergreens and red carnations, and brought back two ruby-colored martinis, handing one to Cici and one to Bridget. "We know," he replied, returning with Lindsay's glass, "that he can fix anything, paint anything, hang anything, and chop anything. And he's Australian! He works every single day from dawn to dusk, and every time we try to pay him he just waves it away, saying he won't take a penny until the job is done. Of course," Paul added with a small uncertain frown, "we expected the job to be over long before now, but it seems as though every time he gets ready to leave, something else breaks. Why, only this morning . . ."

He broke off as Derrick came in, looking harried. "Crisis in the kitchen," he said. His expression cleared when he saw the ladies. "Look how pretty you all are! Where's Lori? Kevin?"

"What crisis?" demanded Paul.

Derrick turned back to him. "Purline has misplaced the crepe pans," he said. "She's threatening to serve cherry puree over sponge cake."

"*My* crepe pans?" demanded Paul. "But I got those in France! It took fifteen years to get them perfectly seasoned! They're irreplaceable."

"I know," replied Derrick soothingly, "you've mentioned that once or twice. I'm sure they'll turn up, but in the meantime . . ."

"Cherries jubilee," suggested Bridget. "Do you have brandy?"

Paul gave her a dry look. "Oh, please, do we have brandy." Then he kissed his fingers to her before hurrying out of the room. "Brilliant idea, though. You are a treasure!"

Bridget felt a tug on her skirt and looked down in surprise to see a dark-eyed young girl in a red wool dress gazing solemnly up at her. "Well, hello there!" she said, smiling. "What's your name?"

"Oh, dear," Derrick said. "This is Purline's little girl. She's not supposed to be in here." He patted the top of her head awkwardly. "She's adopted. From Honduras."

All three women said, "Ah." And nodded in relieved understanding. They, like Paul and

Derrick, had been speculating for months how Purline could have school-age children at her age, and Bridget had even gone so far as to worry about underage marriages and white slavery.

Now Bridget's smile broadened as she said to the child, "Well, you certainly are a pretty thing."

"She's also not supposed to be in here," Derrick repeated, forcing a smile of his own. "Are you, my dear?"

The little girl continued to gaze at Bridget. "My mama says treasure is what the wise men brought to baby Jesus."

The three women smiled the way women do when children are around, and Derrick said, growing ever more agitated, "Your mother also said you were to sit quietly at the kitchen table and study your Sunday School lesson until your daddy gets here. I heard her."

"Mr. Paul says treasure is worth a lot of money," the child added solemnly.

Cici chuckled. "He would."

Bridget gave Cici a look of mild reprimand. "Yes," she told the child sagely, "they both are exactly right."

"You don't look like treasure," said the child.

Lindsay and Cici smothered laughter in their drinks, and Derrick said with forced cheer, "All right, little one, I think that's quite enough adorableness for now." He took her shoulders and turned her back toward the kitchen. "Go find your mother and remind her that you are not allowed around the breakables."

"Mama said for me to find you," replied the child, planting her feet. "Because I'm the oldest."

Derrick looked at her cautiously. "Oh?"

She nodded. "She said to find you and tell you thank you for letting us work here this week. She said to tell you we'll be back tomorrow, but Grandma's coming home on Wednesday. My daddy's here now. Bye!"

The three women stared at Derrick as she scampered off. Cici said, eyebrows raised, "Purline's children are *working* for you?"

He waved a dismissing hand. "It's a long story. They want to buy a goat. Purline has been bringing them to work with her while her mother has surgery—or goes to Arizona, I forget which—and I suppose they're nice enough, very well mannered, but I declare they've worn my nerves to a frazzle. This house is filled with valuables, you know, and children are . . . well, children. I just thank goodness they're going to be gone before our guests arrive."

Lindsay said, "Oh, for heaven's sake, Derrick, you're just an old fuss-budget. I thought she was cute as pie. Aren't there two more?"

"Twins," admitted Derrick glumly. "Boys. They're bound to break something. How can they not? They're boys."

Bridget laughed as she slipped her arm through

his. "You're looking at it all wrong, Derrick. Christmas is all about children. You're lucky to have them here!"

"Think of them as accessories," suggested Cici.

"And they're so much fun to shop for," agreed Lindsay. "What are you getting them for Christmas?"

Derrick, who was still pondering the notion of children as accessories, looked confused. "Oh dear. I suppose we should get them some little trinket. That's what people do when there are children involved, don't they? A dolly, or a book or . . . of course, I'm not certain the little ones can read."

"My grandchildren love their Wii," Bridget suggested.

"It's a video game thingy," Lindsay explained before he could question. "How old are these kids, anyway?"

"Not very old," Derrick replied, looking distracted. "They're children. I suppose we can find something online."

Cici said, "You should probably ask Purline what they want for Christmas. That way you don't get something they already have."

"That's a good idea," Derrick agreed, then sighed. "And I was so proud that all of our Christmas shopping was done."

Then he brightened. "Did Paul tell you we hired that fellow Mick? He's Australian. I can't imagine how he found his way to our shores, can you?"

Cici said flatly, "No, I can't. And it seems to me that might be at least one of the things you should have asked him before you gave him the run of the house."

"We hardly gave him the run of the house," Derrick protested. "Maybe the garage, and the toolshed, and the storage room . . . and the front washroom, which had a leaky faucet, and the Rose Room, when the chimney flue was stuck—disaster narrowly averted, there—and anyway . . ." He looked at Cici hopefully. "We thought you sent him."

Her lips tightened with reproof as she shook her head. "Derrick, just because you're in the country doesn't mean you can abandon your common sense. Paul said he just drove up out of nowhere looking for work."

"Rode," corrected Derrick. "He rode up. On a Harley."

Lindsay and Bridget exchanged an alarmed look, and Cici cast a helpless glance heavenward.

Derrick said, "You may be right. It's just that with all we have going on over the holidays he really was a godsend, and it just didn't seem wise to look a gift horse too closely in the mouth, if you know what I mean. He really can do anything. As a matter of fact," he added on a note of brave resolve, "we're talking about asking him to stay on even after the holidays. A jack-of-all-trades is exactly what we need around here."

"Are you talking about that fellow Mick?" Dominic came up from behind them and rested an affectionate hand on Lindsay's shoulder blade. They were still newlyweds and at the stage where touching each other was as automatic as breathing. "I was just talking to him. Seems like a real stand-up guy. Has some interesting stories, too. He used to tag sharks in Indonesia, and raced the Baja 1000 last year."

"There," declared Derrick, relieved. "What more do you need to know? And Dominic thinks he's a stand-up guy. Dominic, let me get you a drink. Ladies, have you met the Watersons?"

Lindsay stared at her husband. "Tag sharks? Why would anyone want to do that?"

"Oh, and there's Louella Timpson," Derrick added, expertly steering the ladies toward the group by the fireplace. "Come, sit down, have a chat." He raised his voice a little and waved to Louella Timpson. "How are you, my dear?" He bent his head close to Cici's and added, sotto voce, "Don't say anything about her hair. Bad dye job at Missy's Cut and Curl. She's very self-conscious about it." Then, turning toward the door, he called cheerfully, "Welcome! Lovely to see you! Come in, come in. Let me get you a drink. Your table will be ready momentarily."

The ladies, looking only slightly less concerned than they had a moment ago, watched him bustle off.

"Seriously," Lindsay demanded of Dominic. "Sharks?"

"It's a conservation thing," he assured her. "Very noble."

"I don't see anything noble about conserving sharks," Lindsay replied with a frown.

"I don't mean to be a mother hen," Cici said, "but I can't help worrying about them. Paul and Derrick can be a little naive."

"They have the biggest hearts in the world," agreed Bridget, "but they're not always the best judges of character."

"To be fair," Lindsay admitted, a little reluctantly, "we weren't all that sure about Purline at first, either. And she turned out okay."

"She did lose the crepe pans," Bridget could not resist pointing out.

"And nobody liked Harmony when she turned up here, either," Cici added.

Lindsay frowned. "Well, the jury is still out on her."

"Ladies." Dominic placed one hand on Cici's back and the other on Bridget's. "You'll forgive me for pointing out the obvious but . . ." He glanced around the room in a meaningful way. "The gentlemen seem to be doing rather well for themselves. Perhaps, in the spirit of the holidays, you might give them the benefit of the doubt?"

Lindsay's lips turned down in rueful amusement. "You're only saying that because Paul told you where he keeps the key to the wine cellar."

Dominic's eyes twinkled and he dropped a light kiss atop his wife's hair. "Which is where I'm headed right now. Go and talk to Louella Timpson. But," he advised with a perfectly straight face, "don't say anything about her hair. She's sensitive."

The three women watched him go with universal affection. "You know," said Bridget, sipping from her glass, "he's right. We're just being overprotective."

"We should be so lucky as Paul and Derrick," agreed Cici.

"They have everything under control," said Lindsay with a definitive nod of her head.

Bridget said, "And as soon as Kevin gets back from vacation I'm going to ask him to check out this Mick fellow."

The three women, relieved, raised their glasses to that.

NINE

The Spirit of Christmas

Wreaths were hung, trees were decorated, lights were strung. Gingerbread baked in the oven and wassail simmered on the stove, filling the air with the aroma of Christmas spices. Every surface sparkled. Fires were laid in each guest room, awaiting only the strike of a match, and the London Symphony Orchestra's recording of *The Nutcracker Suite* wafted softly from speakers throughout the public rooms. A framed copy of the dinner menu was artfully placed on every dressing table, and on each bed, in a leather bound commemorative folder, the day's agenda was printed in scroll font on heavy vellum paper. No detail had been overlooked, from the cut-glass canisters in the bathrooms filled with lavender scented cotton balls, to the fragrant basket of evergreens and cinnamon sticks that flanked the front door. This was the moment everyone at the Hummingbird House had been working for, planning for, and waiting for all year. Their Christmas guests arrived today.

Gift baskets filled with hand-poured chocolates, local cheeses, preserves, water crackers and a bottle of Ladybug Farm wine were thoughtfully placed in each guest room—with the exception of the room the two teenage girls shared, whose basket contained a bottle of sparkling cider—along with complimentary wineglasses etched with hummingbirds, a corkscrew tastefully imprinted with the name and phone number of the B&B, and of course, a copy of the Geoffery Allen Windsor book. Hand-loomed Christmas stockings, one for each guest, were hung above the fireplace in every room, specifically designed to coordinate with the mantelscape, of course. The bins were filled with firewood, the walk was so thoroughly swept it practically gleamed, and even Mother Nature had cooperated with a delicate frosting of snow that dusted the winter lawn and the holly bushes like confectioner's sugar. Everything was perfect. They were ready.

Almost.

Derrick paced back and forth in front of the window in the reception area, the telephone pressed to his ear. "Still no answer," he fretted. "How could she do this to us? How can she not answer her phone?"

"She's in India," replied Paul calmly from behind the big desk. He was intently focused on the display he was creating with an antique wooden train, a sheet of cotton batting and a collection of miniature Christmas trees. "I don't think they have cell phone service at an ashram."

Derrick pocketed his phone, his face a study in

anxiety. "But Mrs. Hildebrand has booked a massage for nine o'clock tonight, and the Mathesons for ten in the morning, and . . . well, we're booked practically on the hour every hour for the whole weekend, and we have no massage therapist! I *knew* this would happen. How could I not know?"

"Relax," replied Paul, tucking a sprig of evergreen beneath the carpet of cotton batting. "Harmony said they'd be here, and they will. It's barely noon, after all."

"How can you be so calm?" demanded Derrick, scowling. "This is a crisis!"

"Oh, I don't know." Paul stepped back to admire his work, smiling. "There's something about seeing this little train that always puts me in a good mood. It's like childhood in a box."

"Did Santa bring you that, Mr. Paul?" inquired a small voice from behind them.

Paul turned, and even the sight of one of Purline's boys in the reception room barely four hours before guests were due did not erase the smile from his face. "Why, yes he did, young Jacob-or-Joshua," he replied. "When I was a tyke not much older than yourself. And he gave it to my father before me and his father before him. It was handmade in Holland almost two hundred years ago, you know, and has been passed down through my family since that time. It's my most precious possession."

"Even more precious than your crepe pans?" Purline came around the corner in her puffy jacket and ski cap, the other twin in tow. Her tone was slightly sarcastic, because Paul never lost an opportunity to remind her of how valuable the pans were, to which she repeatedly replied that the pans were not lost, simply temporarily misplaced amidst all the Christmas falderal, and how many people really liked crepes anyway?

Paul's smile did falter a smidgen then, and he replied archly, "As a matter of fact, yes. You may be interested to know this little wooden train set is worth far more to me than anything else I own, although I do expect to see those crepe pans back on the stove making crepes before the Christmas season is over."

Purline rolled her eyes. "I left ham sandwiches in the fridge for your lunch," she said, "and I put the chicken and wine in the Dutch oven."

"Coq au vin," correct Derrick. "It's called coq au vin. You used the cabernet, didn't you? Not the Riesling we're chilling to serve with dessert?"

"I used the one you opened and set on the counter with a big sign that said 'use this one,'" she informed him. "Just let the chicken sit and simmer 'til you're ready to serve. The gingerbread is cooling, and the bread needs to warm at three hundred for fifteen minutes. Don't forget to take the butter out of the fridge half an hour before supper to let it soften. You sure you don't want me to come back after you eat and clear away?"

"We can put the dishes in the dishwasher," Paul assured her.

"And don't forget to put the tablecloths in to soak," she reminded him. "Anything that gets spilled on them will go hard as clay by the morning, and I don't have all day to be rubbing spots out of your tablecloths."

"We've done this before, Purline," Paul reminded her.

"I wouldn't go," she said, still sounding worried, "but the kids are doing their Christmas pageant tonight, and I've got to finish gluing cotton balls on the sheep costumes. These two are sheep," she said proudly, slicking back a strand of hair on one of the twins, "and Mimi's an angel."

"Not a real angel," piped up little Jacob-or-Joshua. "Just a pretend one."

Derrick looked around nervously. "Where is Mimi, anyway?"

"Getting the kids' coats," replied Purline. She glanced around. "Did them massage people ever show up? You want me to call Holly down at the Cut and Curl? She does a real nice foot rub before she paints your nails."

"I'm sure that won't be necessary, Purline," Paul said quickly, before a horrified Derrick could form a reply.

"Here I am, Mama!" cried Mimi, skipping into

123

the foyer with an armful of coats. Derrick winced as an errant jacket sleeve sent a string of tiny bells on the reception area Christmas tree to jingling. She skidded to a stop beside her mother and stared up at the two men solemnly. "I'm going to be a angel," she said.

"Yes, we heard," replied Derrick with a brief smile, and turned to her mother. "Purline . . ."

"Not a real angel," reiterated a twin stubbornly. "Not like angel man."

Derrick, having drawn breath to address Purline, stopped and looked at him. Paul spoke first. "Angel man?"

"That's what they call your hired hand," explained Purline with an expression somewhere between contempt and suspicion.

"He's got feathers on his arms," explained the other twin.

This time the two men simply turned to Purline and waited for the translation.

"They mean his tattoos," she said. "They're wings. Nasty things." She leaned close to Paul and Derrick and lowered her voice. "You know who else has wings tattooed on their arms, don't you?"

At their confused silence she moved even closer and whispered with a sharp note of satisfaction, "Hell's Angels, that's who!"

Paul and Derrick could not prevent an uneasy glance out the window, where Mick could be seen applying a cement patch to one of the rock walls in the garden that had become a little wobbly in the past day or so. Though they couldn't hear him through the window, they knew he was whistling a Christmas carol, as he always did when he worked. What fascinated everyone in the house, and often caused them to stop what they were doing and simply listen for minutes at a time, was that Mick never whistled the same carol that was being played on the house stereo system, but he somehow managed to maintain his own perfect tune and rhythm with an entirely different song.

Paul turned away from the window and said, with all the conviction he could muster, "People are allowed to have tattoos, Purline."

"Besides," added Derrick, "I don't think there even are Hell's Angels anymore. Not around here, anyway."

"And just how would you know that?" demanded Purline.

"I read it on the Internet."

"Oh, well then." She did not bother to disguise her disdain. "It must be true."

"Anyway," Paul said firmly, "you may as well get used to having him around because we've asked him to stay on through the holiday and chauffeur our guests, among other things. The drivers Harmony suggested have turned out to be less than reliable."

"Just like her massage therapists," Derrick muttered.

Purline gave Paul a skeptical look. "You think them fancy-pants lawyers and doctors and their nose-in-the-air women are gonna get in a car at night with somebody that looks like him? Good luck with that."

Paul glanced out the window again, looking mildly concerned. "You know," he told Derrick, "she may have a point."

"Perhaps a makeover," Derrick suggested. "I think I have an old tuxedo that would fit him. What do you suppose he is, a thirty-six waist?"

Paul looked at him indulgently. "My dear, you are many wonderful things, but a size thirty-six you have never been."

Before Derrick could register a retort, Purline interrupted with, "Well, you two figure it out. I gotta get going."

"Purline," Derrick said, "if you're going by the post office on your way home, I wonder if you'd be good enough to mail some letters for me." He gestured hopefully toward the office.

She said, "Well, all right, but hurry up. I've got a list as long as my arm to get done this afternoon." She turned to her daughter as Derrick led the way to the office. "Help your brothers get their coats on, honey, and wait for Mama on the porch."

She followed Derrick to the office and Paul,

slipping from behind the reception desk, joined them. "Actually," he said, a little anxiously, "there was something we wanted to discuss with you, this being the children's last day here."

"I told you, I'm not working Christmas morning." She took the stack of envelopes Derrick passed to her from behind the desk and glanced through them curiously. "What is all this? Christmas cards?"

"Our annual donations," explained Derrick, "and the last of the gift cards for our friends."

She glanced at him, puzzled. "Gift cards? You mean, like money?"

"Well, yes," said Paul. "So much easier all the way around."

Her frown was clearly disapproving. "That's like paying a bill. What's that got to do with Christmas?"

"We have a lot of friends," Paul told her, in a tone that was only a little condescending. "We couldn't possibly shop for every single one."

She sniffed her disapproval, thumbing through the envelopes. "In my house, it's not about how much you spend, but how much you care. The real presents are the ones money can't buy, that's what I always tell my kids."

Paul and Derrick exchanged another uneasy look, then Derrick opened a drawer of the desk and quickly pulled out a box wrapped in red paper. "Speaking of which," he said. "We, um, got this for the children." He offered the box to her. "We thought you might like to put it under the tree for them since we won't be seeing them again before Christmas."

Purline took the gift hesitantly, her face softening with wonder. For a moment she just looked at the package in her hand, and then she said softly, "Well, if you two ain't just the sweetest things."

Paul and Derrick smiled their satisfaction. "Christmas is about the children," Derrick said.

Paul told her, "It's a video game console. Our friend Bridget said they might like it."

"I hope they don't already have one," Derrick added.

Purline looked up at them, a small frown knotting her brow. "Those things cost a couple of hundred bucks."

Derrick waved a dismissing hand. "Our pleasure."

She began to shake her head. "It's not that I don't appreciate the thought," she said firmly, thrusting the package back at Derrick, "and all the trouble you went to, but you need to take this right back to the store and get your money back. My kids've got no use for such as this."

"Oh, but Purline," Paul assured her, "we have it on the best authority that the games are suitable for all ages."

"We made certain of it," Derrick added confidently.

"In the first place," she continued, still holding the package at arm's length, "we don't even allow our babies to watch the TV. In the second place, it's too much money. Now you take it back and get the boys a couple of picture books, and little Mimi a nice puzzle. Puppies or kittens or something. Here."

She pushed the package into Derrick's chest and he took it reluctantly. Seeing his disappointment, she smiled and patted his arm. "You really are the sweetest things," she said. "And don't you worry about not seeing the kids again before Christmas. Looks like they'll be coming to work with me the rest of the week. Mama's not flying back until Friday." Ignoring the unilateral dismay that crossed her bosses' faces, she held up the handful of envelopes and added, "I'll get these in the mail for you."

She turned and almost tripped over little Mimi, who was standing at the door to the office, watching solemnly. "Didn't I tell you to wait on the porch?" she scolded.

"I did," replied the little girl reasonably. "Now I'm waiting here."

Purline took the child's hand and hustled her toward the door, pausing to glance back over her shoulder with a rueful shake of her head. "Do you know how many goats that thing would buy?" she said, indicating the package still clutched in Derrick's hands. "I swear, you two beat everything."

When they heard the front door close behind her, Paul said, "Well. That was rude."

"She clearly has no understanding whatsoever of the spirit of Christmas," agreed Derrick. He set the package on one of the bookshelves behind him and opened the desk drawer, taking out the colorfully decorated gift card they had intended to present to Purline for Christmas. "What should we do about this?"

"Cash it in, I suppose. I told you we should have just written her a bonus check."

"This seemed more personal."

"Not to her. Apparently the poor thing hasn't a clue as to how the rest of America celebrates the holidays."

Derrick gazed at the gift card thoughtfully. "Well, we have to get her something."

"Do we?" Paul was still annoyed. "She lost my crepe pans."

Derrick gave him a stern look and Paul shrugged uncomfortably. "I suppose we could trade the gift card for merchandise."

"Jewelry," suggested Derrick.

Paul grew thoughtful. "I was browsing online the other day and saw a darling little tennis bracelet."

"Who doesn't like a nice tennis bracelet?" agreed Derrick.

"This one had stones in it. Semi-precious, of course."

Derrick clasped his hands together in delight. "We could put the birthstones of her children in it!"

Paul considered this. "Do you know when the little darlings were born?"

"Easy enough to find out," Derrick said, "since they'll be here every day this week."

They both considered this unhappy possibility for a moment, and then Derrick said, "We'll have to put a rush on the order."

"The company ships overnight," Paul assured him, "and UPS is very good about deliveries this time of year."

Derrick looked thoughtfully at the gift card in his hand for a moment, and then, with a flourish, produced an envelope from his desk drawer. He tucked the gift card inside, scrawled the name of the UPS driver on the outside, and declared, "There! Our Christmas shopping is officially complete."

"Except," Paul reminded him, "for one puppy puzzle and two picture books."

"And, of course, a tennis bracelet," said Derrick.

Paul frowned. "Life is a great deal simpler when you handle it with gift cards."

"So true," Derrick agreed. "But maybe Purline is right. In the spirit of the season, we could try to be a bit more creative."

"Oh, please. Next you'll be telling me it's not the gift but the thought that counts."

"Don't be absurd." Derrick looked insulted. "It's always the gift." Then he shrugged. "At any rate, there's no point fretting about it." He glanced at his watch and frowned. "I'm calling Harmony again."

"I told you, she can't . . ."

He broke off at a sound coming from outside the window, the rumbling and sputtering of an unmuffled engine accompanied by a sound like cow bells clanging up the driveway. The mutual puzzlement in their eyes quickly turned to alarm as they hurried to the window. They pushed back the drapery just in time to see the most peculiar-looking vehicle either of them had ever beheld lumber toward the parking lot of the Hummingbird House.

"What in the world . . . ?" murmured Paul.

It was, in fact, two vehicles. The first one was a tan Blazer, circa 1980, with rust-colored fenders and no hubcaps. Behind it, bouncing like a puppy on a leash, was a cylindrical object that almost resembled an Air Stream camping trailer, except that it was painted from top to bottom in an exquisitely rendered mural of what was unmistakably the Taj Mahal, complete with reflecting pool and gardens. The two men stared, open-mouthed, until, with a screech of worn brakes and a creaking protest from shock absorbers long past their replacement date, the strange contraption came to a halt.

"No," managed Derrick when he regained his breath. "Oh, no. We have a houseful of extremely well-paying guests due to arrive at any moment and we cannot have—I mean, simply can*not* have—a gypsy caravan blocking our entire parking lot. Not possible. No. Not going to happen."

As he spoke he was rushing toward the door, with Paul close behind. "Spirit of the season," Paul reminded him in a singsong voice, and Derrick glared at him as he jerked open the door.

"Excuse me!" Derrick called out, starting down the steps toward the vehicle. "Hello!"

An Asian man in khakis, a Hawaiian shirt and straw hat climbed out of the Blazer, followed by a woman, also of Asian origin, with a sleek dark bob and slender figure, wearing purple harem pants and a peacock-printed kimono. Both smiled broadly when they saw Derrick.

"Excuse me," Derrick said again, rubbing his arms against the cold. "But this is a private parking lot. Are you lost?"

The man bobbed his head in an affable way, still smiling. "Park Sung," he said. He looked at the woman next to him. "Kim Gi."

The woman bobbed her head as well, her smile steady and brilliant.

It took Derrick a moment to understand the introduction. "Oh. Well, Mr. Sung . . ."

"Park," said Paul beside him. "Mr. Park."

Derrick stared at him.

"It's a Korean name," Paul explained, regarding the newcomers curiously. "Korean surnames are always first." He proved it by stepping forward and offering his hand. "Mr. Park," he said, "I'm Paul Slater."

"Paul Slater," repeated Park Sung happily. His accent was so thick it sounded more like "Pawsladder."

"This is Derrick Anderson."

Again the stranger repeated the words, and even Derrick didn't recognize it.

Paul pressed on. "Can we help you with something? You see, we're expecting guests and we really need our parking lot."

"Really," emphasized Derrick. "You see, this is the most important week of our entire business year. We've planned for months, people have paid us a good deal of money, they're coming in from all over the country, we have carolers on the way, and sleighs, and we still have to find a massage therapist, and . . ." He stopped, staring at the two Asian faces which were nodding and smiling happily at him. "You don't speak English, do you?" He turned to Paul in despair. "They don't speak English."

"It would appear not," agreed Paul.

"But they have to leave!" cried Derrick. "Tell them they have to leave!"

Paul gave him a single dry look, then turned back to Park Sung. "You have to leave," he said.

134

Derrick blew out an exasperated breath. "Mr. Park," he began.

"Park Sung." The other man thumped his chest. "Hoppy fee."

Neither Paul nor Derrick could find a reply for that.

Park Sung tried again, more slowly. "Hah. Mo. Nee. Hoppy fee."

A breeze shook flakes of snow from an overhead branch, and Derrick shivered in his Mark Jacobs wool suit. The two newcomers, in their light summer clothing, did not acknowledge the cold.

Derrick said, "I'm sorry, I don't understand."

Park Sung repeated patiently, "Ha. Mo."

"Nee!" exclaimed Paul suddenly. "Harmony!"

"Hahmonee!" cried Park Sung excitedly. He lifted one foot and pointed to it proudly. "Make hoppy fee."

"Happy feet!" Paul turned to Derrick, looking enormously pleased with himself. "Harmony sent them," he said, and waited for comprehension to dawn on Derrick's face. When it did not, he explained, "Our massage therapists!"

Park Sung nodded enthusiastically. "Hahmonee!"

"He makes happy feet," Paul went on, clearly pleased with himself. "Didn't Harmony say he was a certified reflexologist?"

Derrick looked at him blankly for a moment, and then back to the two strangers. "Harmony sent you? To do massages?"

Park Sung beamed at him.

Paul clapped Derrick on the shoulder. "There, you see? You were worried for nothing. Merry Christmas."

Derrick nodded slowly, still looking a little stunned. "Right. Merry Christmas."

Park Sung smiled at them both beneficently. "We Buddhist person," he said.

TEN

Welcome to the Hummingbird House

Four hours later Paul and Derrick flanked the foyer, nervously straightening their cuffs and checking their ties. Behind them, on either side of the gold-lettered door that read "Spa" stood Park Sung and Kim Gi. They had changed into what were apparently their working uniforms: white cotton pants and white wrap jackets, which might have been appropriated from either a chef's locker or a karate school. Their feet were bare. Derrick, worried about the cold floors, and Paul, worried about sanitation, had tried to offer them a variety of slippers and socks, but they had refused all. "It must be a religious thing," whispered Derrick at last.

"Hoppy feet," agreed Paul, sanguine.

Kim Gi held a tray filled with hand-painted ceramic cups of wassail. No one had asked her to do it, and in fact Derrick, not wishing to impose on her good will, had tried to take the tray away from her, but she, with her unwavering cheek-to-cheek smile, was resolute. "It must be a religious thing," Paul had decided, and Derrick uneasily agreed. "I just don't want to be a stereotype," he added. "After all, they're massage professionals."

To which Paul agreed unenthusiastically, "Presumably."

The first airport limousine arrived at 3:45 with passengers Mathilda Hildebrand and Geoffery Allen Windsor, whose flights from different parts of the country had arrived within fifteen minutes of each other. Mick, in motorcycle leathers, tattoos, and big friendly grin, called "Welcome to the Hummingbird House!" as he trotted around to get the luggage from the trunk. Paul and Derrick, who always greeted their guests personally upon first arrival, came down the steps with hands extended.

Mathilda Hildebrand emerged first, a jewel-topped mahogany cane preceding her. She was a straight-backed, elegant woman with a lush chignon of thick silver hair, high cheekbones, and makeup so expertly applied that it seemed to glorify, rather than attempt to disguise, the fine network of lines that mapped her face. She wore oversized amber-tinted glasses, an emerald coat trimmed with red fox at the cuffs and collar, and sleek black suede boots.

Derrick reached her first. "Welcome to the Hummingbird House, Mrs. Hildebrand," he exclaimed. "I trust your trip was pleasant?"

"Dreadful, just dreadful." She grasped Derrick's arm firmly to lever herself out of the car and onto solid ground. "Thank heavens someone's here to rescue me from that awful writer in the backseat. The trouble with writers is they just can't stop talking about themselves, don't you agree?" She shifted her weight to rest one hand on the cane and looked at Derrick assessingly from behind the tinted glasses. "Now who are you, young man," she demanded, "and why should I like you?"

Geoffery Allen Windsor followed her out of the car with a dry smile. "Don't let her fool you," he said. "She doesn't like anyone. Fortunately, her bark is worse than her bite. Isn't that right, Mrs. Hildebrand?"

"Nonsense," she retorted. "I have neither a bark nor a bite, but if I did I can assure you my bite would be nothing to scoff at. I do still have my own teeth, you know, which is something to remark upon in a woman my age."

There was a twinkle in his eyes as Geoffery passed her envelope purse to her with a small, rather courtly bow. "Don't forget you promised to let me escort you to dinner this evening. You didn't finish the story about the reporter and the bullfighter in Madrid."

She gave a small dismissive sniff. "Well, I rather hope to do a good deal better than you by dinnertime."

She frowned abruptly as Mick came abreast of them, suitcases beneath each arm. "What are you doing here?" she demanded sharply.

Derrick, alarmed, drew a quick breath to say something soothing, but Mick paused and smiled. "I'm just here to carry your luggage, ma'am."

She looked him up and down. "You're sure about that?"

His eyes twinkled. "I am."

"Well," she returned, regarding him with narrowed eyes, "you just see that you do, then." She turned away from him and to Derrick she said, "Who did you say you were, my dear? You're not a writer, are you? And how long are you going to keep me standing in the damp and the cold? I'm an old woman, you know."

Derrick bustled her off, and Paul, recovering himself, rushed forward to shake Geoffery's hand. "Mr. Windsor, it's a pleasure to meet you. I'm Paul Slater, we spoke on the phone. Thank you so much for coming. I hope the drive out from the airport wasn't too unpleasant."

He said, "Oh, she's a charmer. You just have to get used to her sense of humor." He smiled, but his eyes looked tired.

Paul took the briefcase that Geoffery carried and led the way toward the house. "Your books arrived earlier this week, and we have over thirty people scheduled to attend the reading tomorrow. I know it's nothing like the crowds you're used to," he apologized, "but it's quite a treat for our little community to have you here. We've put you in the Sunflower Room," he went on, opening the front door and gesturing Geoffery inside. "It gets marvelous morning light."

"Actually," said Geoffery, glancing around

disinterestedly, "I prefer to sleep in. You have blackout draperies, I presume?"

Paul looked momentarily nonplussed. "Well, of course. Whatever you prefer. Breakfast is from six to nine, but of course we'll be happy to make you a bite whenever you request."

"Good," said Geoffery, still sounding less than interested.

"Dinner will be at seven thirty tonight," Paul went on, "served family style, and afterwards caroling and hot chocolate in the gardens. They're really quite spectacular—the carolers, I mean—but do bundle up to enjoy the show. Meantime, I hope you'll join us for wassail and cheeses in the parlor as soon as you're settled in."

By this time they had reached the reception area, where Derrick was introducing Mrs. Hildebrand to the massage therapists. Park Sung and Kim Gi nodded enthusiastically as the older woman rattled off a confident string of Oriental words and Derrick's eyes lit up.

"You speak Korean!" he exclaimed. Then, lowering his voice confidentially he added, "Could you possibly ask them to move their trailer from our parking lot?"

Mrs. Hildebrand accepted a cup of wassail from the tray offered by the persistently smiling Kim Gi and replied, "Nonsense. I don't speak Korean. I thought they were Japanese." She moved off toward her room.

Geoffery took a cup as well, bowed his head, and said, "Domo arigato." To Paul he said, "Thank you, but I'm rather tired. I believe I'll rest until dinner."

Paul and Derrick barely had time to exchange a puzzled shrug before the next limo arrived. Bob and Sheila Matheson were not, as Paul had assumed, young honeymooners, but newlyweds who were slightly beyond middle age and on their second marriage for each. He was comfortably plump and bespectacled, she was obviously no stranger to the gym or to the wonders of Botox. Both seemed cheerful and easygoing, ready to throw themselves wholeheartedly into everything the weekend had to offer.

The Bartletts arrived before the Mathesons had even been properly checked in, a big, messy family whose glassy eyes and rumpled exterior testified to the past two weeks spent in close confines with people they obviously didn't like—each other. Carl Bartlett was so subdued as to almost fade into the background while his wife, Leona, kept running her fingers through her hair and muttering about never being able to get the smell of that car out of her hair. The oldest girl, Pam, had a bizarre haircut that was shaved on one side and fell in a lank purple curtain on the other, while Kelly, the younger daughter, looked almost normal—except for the short shorts, tee shirt and ankle boots she wore in thirty-five degree weather. Both girls were attached to their phones via earphones through which tinny, atonal music could be heard, and their thumbs never stopped texting. They each wore sullen, self-absorbed expressions that appeared to preclude the possibility of their either acknowledging or responding to the spoken word. Twice Paul had to remove a cup of strongly alcoholic wassail from the teenage Pam's hand and replace it with spiced cider, and he was mightily glad to see the Bartlett family settled in their suite.

Angela Phipps was a lovely blonde-haired woman with faded denim eyes and a quiet grace that somehow seemed designed to complement the tired, automatic smile that continually flitted across her face. She wore a sensible London Fog and Burberry plaid scarf for traveling, and beneath it wool slacks and a pink cashmere sweater. By the time their limo arrived at five o'clock, it was almost twilight, and a light misting snow drifted through the air, catching the twinkling lights that decorated the house and surrounding bushes like dancing fireflies. Her husband Bryce, a good-looking, well-tailored man of distinguished bearing and a quiet expression, offered his hand to assist her from the car, but she just sat there, staring out at the snow.

Mick, with one of their cases under each arm and snow mist sheening his face and hair, paused to smile down at her. "Everything okay, Mrs. Phipps?"

She blinked, and the automatic smile stretched her lips and was gone. "Fine. Thank you for asking." She placed her hand in her husband's and climbed out of the car. "It's all quite lovely, isn't it? Just like a postcard."

She started toward the steps, then glanced back at Mick, a small line of puzzlement between her eyes. "Excuse me. You look familiar. Have we met?"

His eyes twinkled. "I shouldn't be a bit surprised, a lovely lady like you and myself, known to have an eye for such things. There's a little club in Perth I used to frequent in the nineties. Did we tango?"

She laughed, and her husband, glancing down at her, looked surprised, then he smiled. She said, "No, I don't think so."

He smiled. "Then it's my loss." He gestured the two of them to precede him. "You're in the room with the purple door. Your bags will be waiting for you there."

"Mr. and Mrs. Phipps, welcome!" Paul hurried down the steps with an umbrella to shield against the mist. "Mind your step, now. You look chilled. Mick will light the fire in your room straight away, but in the meantime we have hot drinks and snacks waiting for you. Come in, come in."

By the time the last arrivals crossed the threshold at six fifteen, the public rooms of the Hummingbird House were brilliant with lights

144

and chatter as guests wandered from their rooms to gather around the fire, admiring the Christmas trees, sipping wassail and tasting the cheeses. It was, for the most part, an amenable group, although in an ideal world, Geoffery Allen Windsor would have joined them and the two sullen texting teenagers would have stayed in their rooms.

William and Adele Canon arrived on a breath of winter air, rosy-cheeked and laughing and clearly ready to enjoy their holiday. "What a darling place!" exclaimed Adele. "I love it, I just love it! But how on earth did you arrange for the snow?"

"We had to order it in July," Derrick confided as he helped her off with her coat, and she burst into more laughter.

"You're darling!" she declared. "Isn't he darling, Will?"

Paul came forward. "Welcome, Mr. and Mrs. Canon! Come in by the fire and have something to drink." He extended an arm to usher them forward. "Let me introduce you to our staff. You've met our man, Mick? If you need anything at all, he's your fellow. And here we have Park Sung and Kim Gi, specialists in reflexology and Oriental massage. Of course the steam room and the hot tub are available twenty-four hours, but we do ask that you book your massage time the night before . . ."

"Hold on there, young fella!" William Canon

145

had a genial manner and a booming voice that echoed even over the sound of music and voices. "All I want to know is where the first hole is!"

Paul hesitated. "The, uh . . . ?"

"That's what I came here for, isn't it? To play golf?"

When Paul, completely nonplussed, just stared at him, the other man gave a big roaring laugh and slapped him on the shoulder so hard that Paul staggered. "Got you with that one, didn't I, old boy?"

Paul smiled weakly, and Adele Canon gave her husband a look of affectionate exasperation. "Oh, Will, really. It's never funny."

From behind them a female voice, rich with disbelief, said, "Will? Adele?"

Sheila Matheson stood at the door to the parlor, a cup of wassail in her hand. Her husband came to stand beside her, and his smile faded when he saw the newcomers. "Adele," he said flatly. "Will."

It seemed to take a moment for Adele to find her voice. "Bob," she said. Then she looked at his wife. "Sheila."

For the longest time the two couples just stared at each other, and the tension that crackled between them was palpable. Derrick instinctively moved between them, trying to find a smile. "You know each other?"

Will said, without expression, "You could say that. I was married to Sheila for twelve years."

Bob Matheson said, "And I was married to Adele for twenty."

Adele Canon did not take her eyes off the other woman. "I thought you were on your honeymoon."

"We are," replied Sheila. "I thought you were skiing in Maine."

"We were," answered Adele. "Now we're here."

The stare-down went on another beat. Paul rubbed his hands together nervously. "Well," he began, forcing enthusiasm. "What a coincidence."

"It certainly is," replied Adele, still staring at the other woman. "You said you were going to cancel your reservation."

Sheila's husband slipped his arm around her waist. "We changed our minds." He looked at Will. "You said you were going to be in Palm Springs."

"Changed our minds."

"Well, for heaven's sake," exclaimed Sheila, moving forward. "Why in the world didn't you say something? We could have driven down together!"

The two women embraced, laughing, and the two men shook hands heartily. "Will Canon, you old so-and-so, every time I see you, you look younger!"

"You keep promising me that round of golf, but somehow you never come through."

"That's because I've got better sense than to play with somebody who's got nothing to do but work on his game. You skunk me every time."

Adele said to Sheila, "Love your hair! Who did the highlights?"

And Sheila replied, "David Lee, he's an absolute genius and charges for it too. Did you get the pictures I e-mailed you of Glenda and the baby?"

"No, I didn't. When did you send them?"

"Never mind, I have them on my phone."

While Sheila searched through her purse for her phone, Paul and Derrick looked from one to the other of them, baffled. "Well," Paul said at last, a little weakly. "Isn't this nice?"

Adele grinned. "This must seem odd. I sent Sheila the link to your website months ago, before we'd even made a reservation."

"We thought it'd be fun to spend the holidays together," Sheila went on, "but then we never could get our schedules straight."

"But it turns out we did!" Adele said, beaming, and added to their hosts, "Sheila's my younger sister."

"And Will and I were business partners for twenty-five years," added Bob, grinning.

"Until Pinnacle Records bought us out," Will said. "I stayed on a few years as CEO, but it just wasn't the same without my old bud."

"We're both too damn rich," agreed Bob. "Takes all the fun out of working."

"Just because we married the wrong person

the first time around doesn't mean we can't still be friends," said Sheila, thumbing through the pictures on her phone. "We just don't get to see each other as much as we'd like."

"Which is probably why we're all still friends," said Adele, laughing.

"Oh, wait, here they are!" Sheila held up the phone and everyone crowded around to see the pictures.

"Well," Paul said, "Mr. and Mrs. Canon, you're in the rose room. Your bags are already there if you'd like to freshen up. Dinner is in half an hour."

"I'll just go check on it," Derrick said hurriedly.

"I'll help," Paul added. "Please enjoy the refreshments and, um . . . well, welcome to the Hummingbird House."

But none of the four laughing people in the foyer even noticed when they were gone.

The snow shower lasted just long enough to add a fresh glisten to the gardens, which were spectacularly lit by pink, blue and white lights that twinkled from the trees and adorned the low shrubs. Flickering candle luminaries marched along the rock walls and lined the paths that meandered throughout the night garden. Outdoor heaters blew warm air across the upper patio, and a fire crackled and snapped in the stone fire pit at its center, sending orange and red cinders into the air which exploded against the night sky like miniature fireworks. It was here that everyone gathered, sipping hot chocolate spiked with Kahlua and rum and slathered with thick whipped cream, while silver-voiced carolers in Dickensian costumes performed their concert in front of a cascading waterfall fountain where a perfectly animated, multicolored fiber-optic hummingbird fluttered its wings and dipped its head to drink. Wives leaned their heads contentedly against their husbands' shoulders or wound their gloved fingers around a loved one's arm. Mrs. Hildebrand, securely seated and bundled against the chill, sipped her chocolate and applauded by banging her cane on the stone floor, and even Geoffery Windsor, who had emerged from his room just as everyone was being seated for dinner, could be seen to smile in the glow of the firelight. The two mopey teenagers, whether by choice or command, did not attend the festivities, and no one, least of all their parents, seemed to mind.

Paul and Derrick, having made certain everyone had a full mug and was enjoying themselves, stood toward the back, benignly gazing over the results of all their hard work. "There were a few close calls," admitted Derrick beneath the cover of a beautifully rendered a cappella version of "The First Noel." "But all in all, I'd say so far, so good."

"I thought we were done for when Mrs. Hildebrand threw that Bartlett girl's phone in the punch bowl," Paul said with a barely repressed groan.

"*I* thought the whole room was going to stand up and applaud," said Derrick. "I almost did, myself." He sipped his chocolate and added, "To be fair, she didn't so much throw it as drop it."

The incident to which they referred had occurred as Paul was ushering everyone to dinner. The two girls, still dressed in their rumpled traveling clothes and with eyes and thumbs still glued to their phones, reluctantly shuffled toward the door. Their father said something about putting away their phones during the dinner hour, and their mother, who had had several cups of wassail and a glass of wine, waved a dismissing hand. "Oh, please darling, let sleeping dogs lie. We'll all be much happier that way."

Carl Bartlett frowned. "It's rude."

His wife moved ahead of him toward the dining room without giving any appearance of having heard. He tried again. "Pammie, Kelly, we've talked about this. Phones down during dinner."

To which Pamela only rolled her eyes and Kelly, the youngest one, didn't even reply. It was about that time that Mrs. Hildebrand came abreast of the girls and, with a deft backward movement of her cane that caught the cord of Pamela's earbuds, jerked them out of her ears and the phone out of her hand, sending the phone sailing into the bowl of wassail punch on the table. Pamela shrieked.

Mrs. Hildebrand smiled. Everyone else, stunned, simply stared.

"You did that on purpose!" Pamela cried, outraged. She fished the phone out of the bowl with her fingers and cried, "It's ruined, it's ruined!" while Paul rushed to mop up with a napkin the wassail that was dripping on the floor. She whirled on her father. "Did you see that? She did it on purpose!"

To which Carl Bartlett replied mildly, "No, actually, I didn't see a thing." And he, too, moved toward the dining room.

Pamela turned back to Mrs. Hildebrand, her eyes furious and her color high. "You can't do that! You can't just destroy other people's private property! There are laws! You'll see! You can't do this!"

The older woman smiled and patted Pamela on the arm. "Of course I can, my dear. I'm old and I'm rich. I can do just about whatever I want."

She looked then at Kelly, who quickly jerked the earbuds out of her ears and stuffed her phone in her pocket, then hurried to join her parents in the dining room. Mrs. Hildebrand followed at a more leisurely pace, an expression of intense satisfaction on her face.

"I've heard that placing a cell phone in a bowl of rice will dry it out," volunteered Derrick now, as the carolers segued into "It Came Upon a Midnight Clear."

"Yes," agreed Paul, who knew perfectly well there was a five-pound bag of rice in a canister in the pantry. "We must remember to ask Purline where she keeps the rice in the morning."

"We have a new policy, by the way," said Derrick.

"No children under twenty-one?"

"Right."

"Can you believe the Mathesons and the Canons?" murmured Paul in a moment, repressing a shudder. "For a moment I was certain we were in for the War of the Roses."

"It does look as though one of us might have uncovered the fact that they were related," admitted Derrick, mildly disturbed. "Or at least former business partners."

"We'll definitely have to be more careful in the future," agreed Paul.

"Of course, all is well that ends well."

They listened to the remainder of the carol in contented silence.

"That Geoffery Allen Windsor is an odd duck," observed Paul when the carolers launched into the upbeat tempo of "Sleigh Ride" that suggested they were nearing the end of the concert.

Derrick shrugged. "All writers are."

Paul slanted him a mildly offended look. "I'm a writer."

"So you are." Without further clarification, he went on, "At least everything worked out with the massage therapists. Mrs. Hildebrand said her massage was better than anything she's had in San Francisco or New York, and has booked a reflexology treatment for the morning."

"They do seem very eager to please," Paul agreed, "although the language barrier is a problem. I just wish we could have gotten them to come into the kitchen and eat something. I don't like to think of them going hungry when we have all this food just a few steps away."

"It's probably a religious thing," Derrick said, although he, too, looked worried. "Maybe they're vegetarians."

"We have plenty of salad."

"We should take them some," decided Derrick. "Do you suppose they'll be warm enough in that contraption of theirs? We'll take blankets too."

"Well, mates, what do you say?" Mick clapped a hand on Paul's shoulder, his expression cheerful in the firelight and his voice warm. "Shall I toss on another log to warm the night, or let her fade away like the last notes of that lovely choir?"

Paul said. "Thank you for staying to tend the fire, Mick, but you can let it die now, don't you think? Did you get dinner?"

"I did, indeed, and I come bearing gifts." He offered a plastic plate wrapped in tinfoil to Derrick. "From our Korean brethren, as a thank you for your hospitality."

Derrick shuffled his mug to the other hand to accept the plate and carefully peeled back the foil, his eyes widening in delight as he caught the aroma. "What is this?"

"Only the best Korean barbecue it has ever been my pleasure to wrap my mouth around," replied Mick.

"Oh my," said Paul appreciatively as Derrick waved the plate beneath his nose. "And we were worried about what they were having for supper. Wait," he said, and looked at Mick. "You speak Korean?"

"A mite," admitted Mick.

Derrick said eagerly, "Can you tell them to move their trailer? You see, we have sleighs and window vans coming, and we really need our parking lot back."

Mick burst into laughter as the carolers began the first round of "Jingle Bells." "Not a chance, my brothers," he said, and rested a hand on each of their shoulders in a companionable fashion. "Not a chance in this world. Come with me."

The glow from the parking lot reached them before they even rounded the corner of the building. The silver trailer and the battered Blazer were still there, only now they were outlined top and bottom in multi-colored Christmas lights. A dining canopy had been set up outside the trailer and it, too, was draped with red, blue, yellow, white and green lights. Beneath it was a cooking fire and several pots, from which emanated a variety of enticing aromas, with two lawn chairs drawn up around it. A thick orange extension cord ran from the trailer to an outdoor outlet on the side of the Hummingbird House.

Park Sung and Kim Gi, now back in their casual attire, stood and bowed, grinning broadly, when they saw the three men approach. Paul and Derrick waved back weakly, their eyes transfixed by the spectacle. "Quite something, isn't it?" said Mick.

"Yes," managed Paul. "It is."

Most amazing of all, they had somehow managed to outline the mural of the Taj Mahal in tiny white lights so that it looked as though it was alive: the minarets glowed, the reflecting pool shimmered, and the stars seemed to twinkle in the sky.

"Well for heaven's sake," murmured someone behind them, "will you look at that?"

Paul glanced over his shoulder to see that the guests had followed them around the building and now stood, as transfixed as they were, by the sight. Someone else said, "Who needs the tour of lights? I don't think anything we're going to see will outdo this."

Added another, "You gents don't leave any stone unturned, do you?"

Derrick and Paul lifted their cups in salute to the smiling and bowing couple at the trailer, and the carolers began, "We Wish You a Merry Christmas."

"Like I said," repeated Derrick, "all's well that ends well."

December 22

Welcome to the Hummingbird House! Remember if there is anything we can do to make your stay even more delightful, you have but to ask. Directions to nearby attractions, horseback riding facilities, shopping and hiking trails are available at the front desk.

Your hosts,
Paul and Derrick

6:00– 10:00 a.m.	Coffee and pastries available in the dining room
8:30 a.m.	Country breakfast is served in the dining room
1:00 p.m.	A light buffet lunch will be available in the dining room
2:30 p.m.	Reading and book signing by Geoffery Allen Windsor, author of *Miracles for the Modern Age*
4:00 p.m.	Cocktails and hors d'oeuvres served around the Christmas tree in the front parlor
6:00 p.m.	Sleighs begin to load for our gala excursion to the top of Leaning Rock, where you will enjoy an elegant

champagne supper and all of nature's glory beneath a once-in-a-lifetime meteor shower

If you have reserved a spa treatment, your appointment time reminder card is enclosed.

ELEVEN

We Need a Little Christmas

Almost fifty people crowded the dining room of the Hummingbird House for the Geoffery Allen Windsor reading. Paul and Derrick rushed around like pleased parents at a child's birthday party with trays of apple cider and cookies, trying to find folding chairs and cocktail napkins. At precisely two thirty, Paul went to the scrolled antique dictionary stand they were using as a lectern and introduced the writer in glowing prose and stentorian tones. The applause rattled the rafters when their guest of honor at last took his place behind the lectern.

Some of the crowd spilled out into the hallway, where there was standing room only. Cici, who had driven Ida Mae to the event, stood at the back of the hall with Paul and Derrick. "Congratulations," she whispered. "Quite a turn-out."

Derrick rubbed his hands together excitedly. "It is nice, isn't it?"

"Of course," worried Paul, "we weren't expecting quite this many people. I would have borrowed some chairs if I'd known."

"Ida Mae said they announced it in church Sunday," Cici said.

"Ah," said Derrick, nodding. "That's probably Purline's doing."

Purline had made it a point to finish her morning chores in record time and make certain the children had finished theirs as well so that they all could attend the reading because, as she told the children, "the Bible's not the only good book, you know."

Paul said, "I'm glad Ida Mae was able to come. It's good to see her out and about."

"It's good to *have* her out and about," Cici said adamantly, and then lowered her voice as disapproving heads turned in her direction. "She's never been in such a mood as she's been about that damn recipe," she went on. "You know how obsessive old people can be when they lose something."

"No," replied Derrick with a perfectly straight face, looking at Paul. "I wouldn't have any idea." The missing crepe pans had not turned up, and not a day went by that Paul did not remind everyone of the fact.

Paul scowled at him, "Speaks someone who's been whining about losing a letter opener for two days now."

"That letter opener is eighteenth century," objected Derrick, "I paid a fortune for it at auction."

"Anyway," Cici went on, "I thought this might cheer her up. She's just about to ruin Christmas for all of us, as if things weren't bad enough."

"Well, I for one think it was unforgiveable of those young people to run off to Cabo without you," Paul said, managing to get his outrage across even in a whisper. "I don't care if it *is* their honeymoon. Children are so selfish. After all, they'll have the rest of their lives together, but how many more Christmases can they expect to have with you? Not," he assured her quickly, "that I wish you any bad luck."

Cici let that pass with an unhappy shrug. "It's not just that. Dominic left to spend Christmas in California this morning and Lindsay is a wreck."

"What?" demanded Derrick and Paul echoed in chorus, "What?"

More disapproving heads turned and Paul gestured toward the reception area. When the glass door closed behind them, Cici explained, "You know all the kids were coming in this week to spend Christmas at Ladybug Farm. But Dominic's daughter in California broke her leg and she's all alone, so of course he had to go be with her for the holiday. Her brothers are going to surprise her by flying in for Christmas, so how could Dominic stay here?"

"But why didn't Lindsay go with him?" Derrick asked.

Cici replied, "Well, with Kevin and Lori gone, and now Dominic, someone had to stay and run the winery. We have tours and tastings scheduled right up until Christmas Eve, and, aside from Lori,

Lindsay is the only one of us who's ever led one. Of course, Bridget and I tried to tell her we could manage just fine, but the truth is, a last minute ticket to California this time of year is *so* expensive, and they really couldn't even afford Dominic's ticket." She sighed. "It's just so sad. This was supposed to be their first Christmas together, and Lindsay's trying so hard to be brave about it. But every time you look at her, her eyes get all watery, and it just breaks my heart."

"But your house was so beautiful," Derrick objected, as though that should make a difference.

Paul patted her shoulder helplessly. "That's the saddest story I ever heard."

"I know," Cici said with a sigh. "We had such big plans."

"I wish there was something we could do to help," Derrick said, and then he brightened. "Why don't you all come on the sleigh ride tonight? It's going to be marvelous. Horse-drawn sleighs through the moonlight, across the bridle paths up to Leaning Rock, where an amazing champagne supper awaits. It's just the thing to take your minds off of things, and we have plenty of room in our sleigh."

Cici smiled. "You're so sweet. Thank you, but . . ." Her smile turned regretful. "It sounds like something Lindsay would enjoy with Dominic, and I'm not sure that's the thing to cheer her up just now."

Derrick's enthusiasm vanished. "Oh. I suppose not."

Seeing the disappointment on both men's faces, Cici linked an arm through each of theirs. "Come on, let's go back in and listen to what the miracle guy has to say. I'll tell you the truth, if he can get me home without having to listen to that old woman grouse every mile of the way, that'll be miracle enough for me."

But no miracle was forthcoming, it appeared, as Ida Mae ambled out with the last of the crowd an hour and a half later. "Dry as dust," she complained, disgruntled, when Paul inquired what she'd thought of the speaker. "Rambling on and on about this and that when you could tell by his face he didn't give a flip what he was talking about. I prefer my preachers with a little more fire to them."

"Actually, Miss Ida Mae," Paul started to explain, "Mr. Windsor is not . . ."

But Cici, standing behind Ida Mae, frantically waved him silent. "I think you might have enjoyed him more if you'd turned up your hearing aid, Ida Mae," she suggested.

Ida Mae scowled. "I told you, I got no use for the dad-blamed thing. I can hear you just fine, can't I? A lot better than I want to, most days."

Purline came up behind them, pulling on her parka and red knit gloves. Her three little ones, already bundled up, trailed behind. "Well, I thought he was real interesting," she said. "I got him to sign my mama's book for her. See here, he put her name in it and everything." She opened up a dog-eared paperback copy of *Miracles for the Modern Age* to show them.

"Hmmph," Ida Mae said, peering over Purline's shoulder. "Looks like a bunch of hen-scratching to me." She glared at Cici. "We going home, or what?"

"If you'll wait a minute for some of the traffic to clear out," replied Cici patiently, "I'll bring the car up so you don't have to walk so far." She turned to Paul. "What's with that camp set up in your parking lot, anyway? Are you having a carnival too?"

Paul winced. "Long story."

He looked as though he might go on to explain, but at that moment the door that led to the attic staircase opened behind him and Mick came through, balancing a stack of magazines and newspapers that reached almost to his chin. A few of the magazines on top slid to the floor as he side-stepped quickly to avoid bumping into Paul. "Sorry, mate," he said with a grin. "Didn't see you there."

Today his bandanna skullcap was printed with jolly Santa Clauses, and the chains on his motorcycle boots jingled when he walked. The children grinned when they saw him and called, "Hi, Mr. Angel Man!"

He returned, "Hello, my little cherubs. Ready to lead the way to your mum's car?"

Purline caught the twins by the flapping hoods of their coats as they surged forward, and Paul bent to pick up the spilled magazines. "What's all this?" he asked.

"The kids started cleaning out your attic for you," Purline explained. "It's okay if they take this stuff, ain't it? Recycling'll pay them a penny a pound."

"By all means." Paul lifted an eyebrow, impressed, and returned two magazines to the top of the stack in Mick's arms. "Very clever of them. I like to reward ingenuity."

Mick moved toward the door, and Cici opened it for him. Another magazine slid off the stack and landed at Cici's feet as he edged by. "Oopsy-daisy," he said, and it was such a silly thing to hear coming from a man like him that Cici laughed. She picked up the magazine and was about to return it when Ida Mae snatched it from her hand.

Ida Mae gripped the magazine with both hands and stared at it while cold air flowed in from the open door. "Well, I'll be," she said softly. "I'll just be."

Cici said, "What?"

Ida Mae shook the magazine in front of Cici's face. "*Good Housekeeping*, December 1963! Ain't you got eyes, girl? Look at it!"

Cici did, and so did Purline, and so, crowding over her shoulder, did Paul. For a moment Cici, scanning the colorful headlines and cover photo, did not understand. And then she did. "Christmas Angel Cake," she read, "page forty-two." She grabbed the magazine from Ida Mae and flipped through the pages. Sure enough, there it was, complete with full color photos and a recipe: the Christmas Angel Cake. She stared at Ida Mae. "Are you telling me this is it? This is the recipe we've been tearing the house apart looking for these past two weeks?"

Ida Mae's crevassed face was transformed like a Christmas tree when the lights are turned on. Her eyes actually shone as she retrieved the magazine and hugged it to her chest. "Praise Jesus," she said. "This is it. This is the one. Thank you, Lord."

Cici looked at Paul, her own eyes wide with astonishment. "It's a Christmas miracle," she said.

"Now," Ida Mae declared with a nod of her head that sent her gray curls to bobbing, "we can have Christmas." She poked Cici sharply in the ribs with a boney finger. "What are you standing there for, girl? We got baking to do!"

Geoffery Allen Windsor sat on one of the garden benches, watching the sky turn that peculiar shade of winter lavender that it did when it couldn't decide whether to snow or not, wishing he'd bought a pack of cigarettes at the airport. He hadn't smoked in thirty-five years, but he'd decided Bobbie had the right idea. If you were going to go—and there was little doubt that everyone, inevitably, would—why not go out on your own terms? Besides, smokers had a built-in excuse for going out by themselves and doing nothing at all except being alone. At this stage of his life, that was all Geoffery really asked: to be left alone.

The other guests had already started happy hour in preparation for a cold night of sleighing under the stars. He could hear their muted laughter through the wavy-paned windows of the lodge and smell the warm aroma of the spicy canapés that were being served with drinks by the fire in the parlor. One thing about the Hummingbird House, there was never a lack of good things to eat—or drink.

The signing had been his most successful in over a year. He should have been thrilled. Instead, he had felt skewered by all those hopeful, excited faces, so eager to have something to believe in, so certain that he could supply it. He had felt weighed down by the responsibility, pinioned by lies. When he looked out over the crowd, he saw the man he used to be and was too tired to be any longer. As soon as some of the gaiety died down inside the house, he was going to sneak back to his room and try to find a flight home for tomorrow. He couldn't be around these people anymore. He just couldn't.

Geoffery was cold sitting alone in the garden, and he wished he'd brought a cup of cider, or a glass of scotch, with him. But it certainly wasn't worth going back inside for. All that noise and Christmas gaiety, everyone wanting to congratulate him on the success of the afternoon's reading. He had chosen the B&B for the peace and quiet. He'd done his bit, paid his dues. He'd played the role of Geoffery Allen Windsor to perfection. Now he'd earned his solitude.

That was why, when he heard the crunch of a footstep on the pebble pathway behind him, he got up quickly and walked the other way. He hadn't gone ten yards before he stepped right into the path of a wheelbarrow. The wheelbarrow was filled with firewood, and it was being pushed by the muscular biker-dude-looking man who seemed to be in charge of maintenance around the place. Mick, Geoffery thought he was called.

He drew the wheelbarrow to a stop and declared with a grin, "Caution, good fellow! I don't have a license for this thing."

Geoffery returned an automatic smile and stepped around him. "My fault entirely."

"Ah, going my way, I see."

Mick fell into step beside him with the wheelbarrow rattling along in front, and Geoffery swallowed down his annoyance. He had intended to go the opposite way, in fact.

170

"I'm taking this load here up to the hilltop so everyone will be nice and cozy for their star-gazing tonight. The gentlemen don't take any chances when it comes to everybody being comfortable. You'll be going along, I reckon?"

"No, I don't think so," replied Geoffery. "I'm a little leery of sleigh rides without any snow."

Mick chuckled and agreed, "I thought the same, but the bloody things are ingenuous. They have tractor wheels instead of runners. The horses are real though, I'm given to understand. Should be quite an evening. They're expecting a meteor shower, you know."

"Yes, I know." And although he really didn't feel like engaging in conversation, Geoffery couldn't help adding as he glanced at him, "Do I know you from somewhere? You look familiar."

"Could be," admitted Mick. "You spend much time Down Under?"

"You remind me of that actor, played a street priest on that TV show in the nineties. I think he's dead now."

Mick grinned. "Then I'm probably not him."

They left the hard-packed garden path for the parking lot, and the wheelbarrow wobbled dangerously on the rough gravel. Geoffery grabbed the front to steady it.

"Why, thank you, there, mate," said Mick. "But we can't have a paying guest doing chores."

Already Geoffery regretted lending a helping

hand, because it meant there was no easy way to veer off back to the privacy of his room now. He'd have to walk the man all the way to the truck he could see parked midway down the drive. But he said, "No problem. I've got nowhere else to be."

"Well, you surely were a phenomenon this afternoon. Every soul walking out of there was talking about how much they liked your book."

Geoffery said nothing.

"Of course, I'm not much of a reading man, myself, but I did happen to be passing by during your talk and I liked what you said there, about miracles being all around us. It's a rare thing to meet a believing man these days."

Geoffery said stiffly, "I'm just a writer, Mr. . . ."

"Mick," supplied the other man.

"Right." His back was beginning to ache so Geoffery straightened up, rubbing it. Mick let the wheelbarrow rest. "Well, Mick, like I said, I just write things down. It has nothing to do with what I do or don't believe."

"Is that a fact?"

Mick looked, and sounded, genuinely interested, and it occurred to Geoffery that he probably had never met someone who made his living with words before, which would be a curiosity in itself. This made Geoffery feel a little more generous toward him than he might have been otherwise.

He leaned back down to steady the front of the wheelbarrow and they started bumping across the rough lot again.

"I've written four other books," Geoffery said, "but no one ever talks about those. Good luck even finding a copy of any of them now. That's the business, though. Here today. Gone tomorrow."

"Were they about miracles too?"

They passed the colorful little camp with its extraordinary mural and its neat little outdoor room. The blackened stones of the campfire smelled like spices, and a bright yellow table-cloth, anchored by a blue bowl filled with apples, covered a folding table.

Geoffery said, "They were about different things. One was about a bunch of guys that got lost in the Himalayas and how they survived. Another was about military dogs in Iraq. The point is, nobody asked what I believed when I wrote those books. Nobody cared. You don't have to believe in a thing to write it down."

"True enough, I reckon," agreed Mick amicably. "So what gave you the idea to write a book about such things, then?"

Geoffery hesitated, and almost gave his standard interview answer, the one that began with "I've always been fascinated by the unexplained . . ." and was, of course, complete BS. But it all seemed like too much trouble to make up lies in this quiet lavender twilight, so he decided to tell the truth instead. "It wasn't my idea, it was my wife's. Liz."

They had reached the pickup truck and there was no reason for him to linger, or say any more. He straightened up, rubbed his back again, and couldn't keep the wry and reminiscent smile off his face as he went on, "Now that's a story, the way we met. I wanted to put it in the book, but no one would believe it." That wasn't true. He'd never even considered putting the story in the book, or telling it to anyone who didn't already know it. He wasn't sure why he was doing so now, except that the other man seemed so interested, and was easy to talk to, and having brought the subject up it would be rude not to finish.

He said, "I was pushing forty, still single. My friends were always trying to fix me up, and if you've ever been in that situation you know blind dates are everything they're cracked up to be."

Mick grinned sympathetically and placed an armload of firewood in the truck bed. Geoffery added another couple of pieces to the pile and went on, "My sister had been after me for months to go out with a friend she thought would be perfect for me, but believe me, I'd been burned on that once too often. My sister thought any woman with a pulse was perfect for me. So to get her off my back, I let my dentist set me up with his neighbor for a double date. And wouldn't you know, as soon as we firmed up plans, I met Lizzie on this Internet dating site I'd almost forgotten I was on. Hadn't had a hit in months, and all of a sudden there she was—this gorgeous, smart, professional woman who made me smile with every word she typed. Long story short, we only corresponded for a couple of days and I was smitten. I had to meet this woman. I was headed out of town for two weeks, and I knew I couldn't wait until I got back to ask her out. I'm not proud of it, but I completely blew off the blind date to ask Liz out that night. It turned out her own plans for the evening had been canceled at the last minute, so she was free. It seemed like fate.

"I was like a kid before the prom, getting ready for that dinner. Best restaurant in town, flowers to be delivered at the table, preordered a wine she'd mentioned she liked, I mean I was over the top. And when I got to the restaurant there was a message from Liz, apologizing that she had to cancel. Some kind of work emergency. It served me right, of course, after the way I'd canceled on the other woman at the last minute, but you can imagine my mood as I drove home that night. I didn't even see the car that turned in front of me until it was too late. I swerved and hit a utility pole to avoid him, and next thing I know I'm in the back of an ambulance on the way to the ER. What was supposed to be the best night of my life ended up one of the worst. Or so I thought."

Mick tossed the last log on the pile and glanced at him curiously, waiting. Geoffery smiled.

"The first person I saw when I got to the ER was the charge nurse who checked me in. She was the most beautiful woman I had ever seen, and her name tag read Elizabeth Sumpter. We were married six weeks later."

"Wait," said Mick. "It wasn't the same woman . . . ?"

Geoffery nodded, still smiling. "It was my Liz. She'd had to break our date when one of her nurses called in sick. But she ended up being there for me when I needed her most."

Mick shook his head, grinning. "Well, I'll be."

"That's not even the kicker," Geoffery said. "You know those plans of hers that got canceled at the last minute? Turns out her next door neighbor had fixed her up with a blind date who was rude enough to break it three hours before they were supposed to meet. Her neighbor was a dentist."

Mick gaze grew skeptical. "You never."

Geoffery nodded. "I was the blind date. And two weeks later, when I introduced her to my sister, it turned out there was no need. They'd been friends for ages. In fact, my sister had been trying to fix me up with Liz for months."

Mick was laughing now. "And you say you're not a believin' man? By my teeth, that's the finest story I ever heard. If all the tales in your book are like that one, I might just have to buy myself a copy."

Geoffery's smile faded. "Like I said, that story never made it into the book. But it was because of it—because of Liz—that I wrote the book. A Facebook page, and a question: Has a miracle changed your life? It was unbelievable. We got hundreds of thousands of replies. Some of them were worth an interview. Some of them were worth printing. God, those were the best times." He was back there now, in those days, the days when he never stopped smiling, and his eyes showed it. "Liz was so—I don't know, so *pure*. So purposeful and certain and joyful and intense. She made me believe in impossibilities. And, sure enough, the impossible came true. The book sold at auction for enough of an advance that we could afford to pay cash for a house on the river. It went straight to the top of the *Times* list the week it was released. How does that even happen? I went on tour and the lines were down the street. I was on Oprah and sales went through the roof. I was a rock star, and let me tell you I enjoyed every minute because Liz loved it so much. She kept saying, *I told you, I told you!* As though it was her faith in me—in us, really—that had made it happen. And who knows? Maybe that's what it was. Maybe that's all it ever was."

His smile was gone, and his eyes were bleak. "She was dead before Christmas of that year," he said. "Pancreatic cancer. We had two weeks to say good-bye, and I wasted them praying for a miracle that never came." He lifted his shoulders, and then let them sag in a heavy shrug. "In the book I said that a life without the possibility of miracles is a life that's not worth living. I didn't know at the time how true those words were. Before Liz, there was no magic. After Liz, even the possibility of magic was gone. So." His lips tightened at the corners in the semblance of a smile that held no mirth whatsoever. "Now that you know the end of the story, you'll probably want to save your money on the book."

Mick sat on the open tailgate of the pickup, his expression thoughtful. "Do you know the difference between magic and miracles?" he said. "One of them requires faith." He gave a crooked smile. "My dear ol' mum taught me that, may God keep her in the balm of His grace."

Geoffery replied flatly, "Good to know." He started to turn toward the house, suddenly weary, but the other man's voice stopped him.

"Seems to me that miracles are a lot like stories," he mused. "They're everywhere you look, if you just keep your eyes open. Why, I wouldn't be surprised if you found a half dozen of them right here on these very grounds."

Geoffery gave a half-smothered snort of laughter. "Like the old woman and her fifty-year-old magazine? Believe me, I hear a dozen stories like that every day. Coincidence, random chance, miracle, doesn't matter what you call it. Because in the end the one thing all those stories have in common is that they're pointless. Believe me, both miracles and stories are in very short supply these days."

"Maybe," replied Mick amiably. "But then again maybe the point is not so much in finding the things, but in looking for them. I know I'd surely rather live in a world where people are expecting a miracle than where they're not. Shouldn't be surprised if your wife didn't think so too."

Geoffery didn't know why the reference to his wife, coming from this stranger's mouth in such a casual fashion, should offend him, but it did. He had shared too much. Taken the sacred out of what should have been his last secret. He was disgusted with himself.

"It's cold," Geoffery said stiffly. "I'm going in." He turned toward the house.

Mick nodded sagely. "You were right about one thing, though," he said. "There wasn't an angel at the twin towers."

Geoffery glanced back at him curiously. Mick smiled.

"There were thousands," he said.

It was at that moment that all the lights on the Hummingbird House came on, perfectly coordinated on timers, and Geoffery couldn't help turning to look. The curtain lights, the wreath lights on every door, the colored floodlights and twinkle lights illuminating all the trees and bushes; it really was a fairy-tale moment. It was just mesmerizing enough to catch Geoffery off balance for a second or two, and he simply stood there, watching.

He started up the drive again, but had only taken a step or two before he stopped, frowning. "Wait a minute," he said. He turned. "How did you know I said that?"

There was no answer. He raised his voice. "That thing about the angel. I never said that to anyone but Bobbie. How did you know? Mick?"

But there was no reply, and all he saw was the twin red taillights of the truck disappearing down the driveway.

TWELVE

Sleigh Ride

The two big sleighs, each large enough to hold eight people, were waiting to transport the guests of the Hummingbird House to their fantasy evening of hilltop star-gazing at six p.m. They were elaborately painted in red and gold, and outfitted with plush velvet seats, footrests and running lights cleverly designed to look like iron lanterns. There were faux fur lap throws and hot chocolate for the half-hour jaunt across the countryside, and each team of two horses wore harnesses trimmed with jingle bells and twinkle lights.

Earlier in the summer, Paul and Derrick had read in the local newspaper about the enterprising farmer who'd come up with a way to make money during the winter by offering horse-drawn sleigh rides to tourists—with or without snow—and had been fascinated ever since. They'd made several trips to the farm to inspect the equipment, engaged in lengthy discussions about the venue for and the length of the sleigh tour, whether daytime or nighttime would be best, whether it should be a means of transportation to another event or a destination in itself. When they discovered a meteor shower was expected a few days before

Christmas, the event practically planned itself.

A bonfire was waiting atop the hill, along with cushioned chairs and portable tables set with white linens and crystal, evergreen bouquets, and candles in hurricane globes. Two liveried waiters, excited by the chance for extra holiday cash, warmed their hands over the fire and joked with each other about the way rich folks lived. A cooler was filled with champagne and chocolate truffles; an insulated container held lobster bisque and a steaming cassoulet. It would be an evening like no other, another stellar memory to be pressed into the book of an unforgettable Christmas at the Hummingbird House.

The Mathesons and the Canons shared the lead sleigh with Paul and Derrick, who generously spiced their chocolate with Irish Cream and cinnamon sticks, making for a joyous ride all the way. The Bartlett family shared the second sleigh with the Phippses and Mathilda Hildebrand and—at the last minute—with Geoffery Windsor. The two married couples took the plush, sofa-like seat in the back, leaving Mrs. Hildebrand to groan elaborately as she thumped down beside Geoffery in the front: "God! Again with the writer!"

He smiled back, "Always a pleasure, Mrs. Hildebrand."

Pamela and Kelly Bartlett slumped in at last. Kelly, with her iPad glowing in the dark, hunched far over in the corner, leaving Pamela no choice but to flop down on the seat next to Mrs. Hildebrand. "You owe me eight hundred dollars," said the teenager, glaring at the older woman.

Mrs. Hildebrand balanced both hands on the jeweled head of the walking stick in front of her as the horses lurched forward. "Do I indeed?" she replied pleasantly. "Might I ask for what?"

"You know for what! You ruined my phone!"

Said Mrs. Hildebrand, "And you paid what for it?"

"I told you that."

"No, my dear," the other woman replied patiently. "You told me what your father paid for it, and he doesn't want my money. So in actual fact, you paid nothing for your supposedly damaged property, and that's exactly what I owe you: nothing. Shall we move on?"

Pamela drew in a sharp breath for a reply but clearly couldn't find one. The sleigh bounced sharply, throwing her against her sister, who violently pushed her away. Geoffery said mildly, "Hot chocolate, anyone? I believe there's some in the basket here."

From the sleigh in front of them, there was a burst of laughter. From the seat behind them, which was too high to see over, only quiet polite murmurs of conversation.

Mrs. Hildebrand shot Pamela a sideways look. "Did Aiden Sanders do your hair? He's definitely losing his touch."

Pamela returned a glare. "What would you know about it? You're a million years old."

"Oh, please. Aiden Sanders would still be doing weaves in Birmingham if I hadn't introduced him to Tyra Banks." She turned to Geoffery and added, "Now he owns salons in Richmond, New York and San Francisco, does celebrities on both coasts. But what kind of mother would spend twelve hundred dollars to let him do *that* to her daughter's hair I can't begin to tell you."

Kelly leaned over her sister to stare at the older woman. "You do not know Tyra Banks."

Pamela fingered her choppy lavender hair uneasily, then stopped herself. "Anyway, it wasn't him, it was his new girl, Tempe. And I like it."

"Never go with the new girl, my dear," replied Mrs. Hildebrand. "You'll learn that when you get older. Aiden wouldn't have dreamed of doing purple with your complexion. Indigo, definitely."

Once again Pamela tugged at the ends of her hair.

Geoffery poured chocolate from the thermos into a mug and offered it to the older woman. "Weren't you on safari in Africa with M.C. Hammer last year?"

Mrs. Hildebrand took the mug and sipped from it, aware of the big eyes of both girls staring at her. "That's how I broke my hip, running from that damn rhinoceros."

There was a significant pause, broken only by

jingle bells and the clop of hooves over well-trod terrain. Then Pamela breathed, "You did not."

Mrs. Hildebrand sipped again from her mug. "Of course not, you ignorant child. I broke my hip stepping off a curb in New York. And it was John Legend, not M.C. Hammer, in Africa. We were dedicating a school for girls." Another sip. "An intelligent person might ask why."

The two girls exchanged frowns, clearly debating whether this was another trap. Then Kelly, on a quick impatient breath, demanded, "Why?"

Said Mrs. Hildebrand, "Because if you educate a woman, you educate a village. Bono said that, I believe."

Said Pamela skeptically, "Yeah, like you know him too."

"I do indeed." She glanced down at her mug and made a face. "Is there any scotch in that basket?"

Geoffery checked the basket. "Sorry. Brandy?"

She held out her cup and he splashed a measure of brandy into it. She tasted it critically and then glanced askance at Pamela. "I don't suppose you'd be interested in hearing the story of how we met."

Uncertainly, a little cautiously, and clearly not wanting to appear too interested, both girls leaned in, listening.

In the seat behind them, Leona Bartlett turned off her phone and dropped it into the pocket of her coat.

"Thank you," her husband said.

"I lost the signal," she replied. "Come on, darling, just because we're stuck in the wilderness doesn't mean the rest of the world stops. I've got to keep up with e-mail."

Carl glanced at the couple at the other end of the seat and said, "There's a thermos in the basket here. Can I pour you folks a drink?"

Angela Phipps replied with a pleasant smile, "None for me, thanks." She glanced at her husband. "Darling?"

He said, "No thanks, I'm good." He adjusted the fur throw across his wife's knees with a tender smile.

Leona whispered, "The love birds. It's really a little disgusting, the way they fawn over each other." But she was smiling as she said it.

Carl closed the lid of the hamper and said to his wife, quietly, "Has the trip really been that bad?"

"Oh, please." She slipped her arm through his and leaned into his warmth. "You're not going to pretend you *enjoyed* Florida. The best thing about this family vacation is that it's almost over. I would have rather spent the last two weeks in the pit of hell than in the so-called happiest place on earth with those two demon spawn we're raising as our daughters. And if that phone I ordered for Pammie doesn't get here tomorrow, we're all done for."

"It won't," he assured her. "I canceled the order."

She pulled away from him, staring. "Are you insane?"

He sighed. "I was hoping that without that damn thing glued to her hand she might actually start talking again. Or at least listening."

Leona's eyebrows shot up. "Oh yeah? How's that working out for you?" Then she shrugged and snuggled up to him again. "Anyway, today was nice, wasn't it? The massage was out of this world, and the girls seemed to enjoy horseback riding—well, as much as they enjoy anything that is. And," she added, lowering her voice and squeezing his arm, "they're both sure to say this is the best Christmas ever as soon as they see the diamond watches you got them."

He looked at her, surprised. "How did you know?"

She smiled secretly and pressed her face to his shoulder. "The same way I know you got me that emerald necklace I made such a fuss over when I saw it in the jewelry store window last month. You are the most adorable man. How could I not love you?"

He looked down at her slowly in the dark. "What if . . ."

She tilted her head to him. "What?"

"I just sometimes wonder what would happen if it all went away. The money, the success. The job."

She studied his face. "What an odd thing to say. Do you think we take you for granted?"

"No, of course not."

"Carl?" Her expression grew mildly concerned. "Is something wrong?"

Carl smiled, faintly. "Nothing. Not a thing. Just don't say anything to the girls about the watches, okay? You told me once that a girl never forgets the first man who gives her diamonds, and I wanted that man to be me. So let me surprise them."

"Adorable," she repeated, and laid her head on his shoulder again.

Bryce Phipps said, "Are you warm enough, sweetheart?"

"Umm." Angela leaned into the circle of his arm. "Look at those stars. Gorgeous, aren't they?"

"Reminds me of that camping trip we took in Colorado."

She smiled. "The dude ranch. We were a lot younger then."

"Let's just say I'm glad to be riding in the back of a sleigh, rather than on the back of a horse," he agreed, and she chuckled.

"This has been lovely, Bryce," Angela said. "I'm glad you thought of it."

"Yes, it has been."

"So much better than the same old round of banquets and parties and concerts we do every year."

"It gets old," he said. "It's nice to do something different for the holidays."

They listened to the jingle of bells and clop of hooves for a while, the murmur of the voices of their fellow occupants of the sleigh and the occasional burst of laughter from the sleigh in front of theirs.

"It's all really just charming," Angela said.

"Exactly as advertised," said her husband.

She glanced up at him. "Are you sure you wouldn't like something hot to drink?"

"No, I'm fine. You?"

She settled against his shoulder again. "Just fine."

But she wasn't, of course.

Neither was he.

Paul and Derrick stood a little distance away from the others, contentedly surveying the evidence of yet another successful evening. The bonfire crackled, champagne sparkled, and voices were raised in laughter and conversation. The dinner had been magnificent, and was even served hot. Truffles were passed around with bowls of Bridget's peppermint cream to exclamations and feigned protests and moans of utter delight. The chatter had been lively, sparked by the champagne and the magic of the crisp night air. Everyone seemed to be having a wonderful time.

"We," declared Paul, "are brilliant." He lifted his glass to his partner in salute.

Derrick returned the salute with his own glass. "We're lucky," he corrected. "What if it had rained? Or been too windy to dine outside? Or too cold?"

"Well, it wasn't. Everything was perfect."

"We were lucky," reiterated Derrick.

"You know," Paul said, "we really are. When I think about poor Lindsay . . . well, Cici and Bridget too. They're having a horrible Christmas."

"We'll have them over for Christmas dinner," Derrick decided.

"Of course."

"And we got them each a lovely spa basket."

"We always give them spa baskets."

"And they always love them."

"You know," Paul said thoughtfully, sipping his champagne, "Purline may have a point. Not much of one, mind you, but still, for the people we really love maybe an expensive gift isn't enough. We should try to do something more meaningful."

Derrick seemed perplexed. "More meaningful than spa baskets?"

"I know!" Paul exclaimed suddenly. "We'll call Senator Tarkington!"

"Why?"

"You remember how disappointed Lindsay was that Noah could only have a couple of hours off on Christmas afternoon? Well, what if we could surprise her by getting him leave for the whole weekend?"

Enlightenment dawned, and Derrick grinned.

"Whoever would have guessed that we'd one day be glad to know someone on the Armed Services Committee?"

Paul nodded in pleased satisfaction. "Brilliant," he said.

Derrick clinked his glass against Paul's. "Brilliant."

Someone cried, "Oh, look! There's one!" And they turned to watch the shooting star.

Carl Bartlett came up behind his wife and placed a hand on her shoulder. She lifted her own hand and entwined her fingers through his, nodding toward where their two daughters still sat at Mrs. Hildebrand's table listening to her talk with rapt expressions on their faces. "Darling, hold me," she murmured. "I think I'm about to fall into a parallel universe. Those two are actually having a *conversation*. With an *adult*."

He smiled. "The only stars those girls are interested in are the ones Mrs. Hildebrand knows."

"I'm serious. You may have ruptured the time-space continuum. They seem to be on the verge of discovering that there are other people in the world besides themselves." She finished off her glass. "I need more champagne."

Carl handed her his glass. She leaned back against him and sipped contentedly. Another meteor shot across the sky and a spattering of applause broke out.

Carl said softly, "I love you."

She smiled up at him. "I know."

"It's just that . . ." He hesitated. "I might not get another chance to tell you that." He saw the flicker of alarm in her eyes and corrected himself quickly. "A better chance, I mean, with the stars and all . . . and in all the confusion of Christmas I just wanted you to know that I love you, and the girls, and that it has nothing to do with diamonds and emeralds."

She looked slightly puzzled. "You're acting awfully strange tonight, honey. Are you sure everything is okay?"

He closed his eyes and kissed her hair, and there was a moment when he almost told her everything, right then, right there. But it was just a moment.

He smiled, and told her, "Everything is perfect."

He did not notice that when his wife turned away to watch the next burst of shooting stars, she looked far from convinced.

A few feet away Angela and Bryce Phipps stood with their backs to the crackling fire, cradling champagne glasses in their hands, watching as the streaks of light moved faster and faster across the sky. Bryce said quietly, "There's more for us out there, Angie. More life, more love, more everything. We're both still young. We can start over."

She smiled and lifted her glass as another chorus of oohs and ahhs went up from the gathered watchers. "I can never start over," she said. "There isn't any more for me."

Someone started singing "O Little Town of Bethlehem." Another voice joined in, and another. *Above thy deep and dreamless sleep/the silent stars go by* . . .

Bryce said, "When we get home, I'm filing for divorce."

The hopes and fears of all the years/are met in thee tonight . . .

She said, with no change in her expression whatsoever, "Okay."

She smiled fleetingly at someone who glanced her way, and he put an arm around her waist. They stood together on the top of the hill and watched in silence as the stars fell down.

December 23

Good morning! Just a reminder that for those last minute gifts for those at home, we do offer express shipping service. Leave your properly addressed packages at the desk before 10:00 a.m. and the charges will be added to your bill at checkout. Today is the last day we can guarantee Christmas delivery. Have you done the tour of local antique shops yet? Ask for a list, or see us about arranging transportation. Have a wonderful day in the beautiful Shenandoah Valley!

Your hosts,
Paul and Derrick

6:00– 10:00 a.m.	Coffee and pastries available in the dining room
8:30 a.m.	Country breakfast is served in the dining room
1:00 p.m.	A light buffet lunch will be available in the dining room
2:30 p.m.	Shuttle departs for the tour of the Ladybug Farm winery and cooking class at the Tasting Table
5:30 p.m.	Shuttle returns to the Hummingbird House

6:00 p.m.	Cocktails served in the front parlor around the Christmas tree
7:30 p.m.	Dinner is served in the dining room with a selection of Ladybug Farm wines. Dessert courtesy of Chef Bridget Tindale, your culinary instructor
9:00 p.m.	Vans depart for a tour of the spectacular holiday lights of nearby Evergreen Park

THIRTEEN

Change of Plans

"Well, will you look at me?" Mick grinned as he admired himself in the cheval mirror that stood against the office wall, turning in profile and then back again. "Wouldn't recognize myself on the street, would you?"

That was perhaps a slight exaggeration. Derrick's old tuxedo, which was too small at the shoulders and too big at the waist—not to mention the trousers that were tucked into Mick's motorcycle boots as a way of dealing with the fact that the cuffs landed about two inches above the ankles—made him look more like the ringmaster of a very strange circus than the respectable chauffeur Derrick had in mind. Derrick stepped back, eyeing his creation critically.

"I don't know," he said. "Something's not quite right. Perhaps different headgear?" He indicated the bandanna that was tied around Mick's head above the long braid—blue, today, covered in white snowmen wearing green holly wreaths.

Paul came into the room, stopped a foot or so inside the door, and did a double take. Mick spun on his heel and swept a bow. "What do you think, then? Magnificent, eh?"

197

Paul replied, "Um."

Mick turned back to the mirror and adjusted his bow tie. "I was a stranger and you took me in," he said, grinning at them both in the reflection of the mirror. "I was hungry and you fed me, I was naked and you clothed me . . . You, my brothers, are the genuine article, aren't you?"

"Well," said Paul, still staring at him with an expression of stunned disbelief.

Derrick met Paul's gaze and returned a helpless shrug.

"Well then, I'd best go polish up the van if I'm going to be driving those fine ladies and gents to cooking class today, yes? And the perfect chance to show off my new togs!" He slapped Paul on the shoulder in passing and was whistling "Jingle Bells" in perfect counterpoint to Manheim Steamroller's "Carol of the Bells" that came through the wall speakers as he left the office.

Paul looked at Derrick and said simply, "Seriously?"

"I did the best I could," replied Derrick defensively. He plucked the dressmaker's pincushion off his wrist and tucked it, along with the tape measure he had draped around his neck, into his desk drawer. "And I still think a change of headdress would make all the difference. By the way," he added, "thank you for returning the children's video console. I was going to package it up for today's UPS pickup, but you'd already done it."

Paul said, "I didn't return it. You know I leave that sort of thing to you."

Derrick frowned, confused. "How odd. Do you suppose Purline . . ."

There was a tap on the door and Geoffery Windsor looked in. "Excuse me, gentlemen."

"Mr. Windsor," Paul greeted him warmly. "How are you enjoying your stay? Do you have everything you need?"

Geoffery came in the room and said, "Everything has been fine, just fine. However, I wanted you to know I've decided to cut my stay short."

"Oh, no." Derrick's crestfallen expression was somewhere between anxiety and deep concern. "Is everything all right? There hasn't been bad news, has there?"

"Is it something we've done?" offered Paul. "Something we didn't do? Because believe me, our only desire is to make every guest at the Hummingbird House feel pampered and at home."

Geoffery raised both hands in protest. "No, no, believe me, my stay has been wonderful. I have every intention of giving the Hummingbird House the highest recommendation to all my friends."

Paul relaxed marginally, though he still seemed confused. "It's just that no one has ever left the Hummingbird House early before."

And Derrick added, "Won't you reconsider? The weekend package was part of your compensation for the reading yesterday, which as you know was a grand success, and I'll feel just awful to think we've shorted you in any way."

Geoffery smiled. "You really are nice," he said, "both of you. And I appreciate your generosity, I do. It's just that it's Christmas, you understand, and I'd like to be at home. I can get a train from Charlottesville tomorrow afternoon that will have me home by dinnertime, so I was wondering if you could arrange transportation into town sometime in the morning."

"Well, of course," Paul said, still a bit uncertain. "No problem at all."

"In fact, the van is taking Christmas shoppers into Staunton in the morning," Derrick added. "If you don't mind a brief stop, our driver will be happy to take you right to the station afterwards."

"Thank you," Geoffery said, "that sounds fine." He turned to go.

"But," insisted Derrick, "you'll at least enjoy the rest of your stay with us, won't you? The winery tour is fascinating, and you'll adore Bridget's cooking class. Even if you can't boil an egg, she'll make you feel like a pro. And," he added with a grin, "you get to eat the proceeds!"

Geoffery said, "I'm sure it'll be lovely, but I prefer to stay here this afternoon and pack."

Paul said, "We'll be sorry to lose you, Mr. Windsor. Please let us know if you change your mind."

When he was gone, Derrick looked at Paul with a resigned quirk of his lips. "Well," he said.

"Indeed," agreed Paul. Then, frowning a little, "Did you hear what he called us?"

"Nice?"

"Exactly."

Derrick frowned as well. "I never thought of either one of us as nice, did you?"

"Absolutely not."

"Erudite, interesting, sophisticated . . ."

"Brilliant," supplied Paul, "witty, charming, urbane . . ."

"Well spoken, compassionate, even generous," added Derrick.

"But not nice," Paul concluded, wrinkling his nose slightly in distaste.

"Definitely not," agreed Derrick.

"At any rate," Paul said, flinging himself onto the leather settee beside the window, "there's more bad news. The president has canceled his holiday trip to Camp David."

Derrick lifted an eyebrow, obviously confused. "I'm so sorry for him. But we seem to have an open room at the Hummingbird House if he needs a place to stay."

Paul deliberately ignored the witticism. "That means all leave in Noah's unit has been canceled," he explained. "Apparently when the president is in town, the Marines are in town, or some such nonsense. Even the senator can't do anything about it."

"Oh, no!" Derrick said, dismayed. "I already told Noah our plans!"

"Well, it doesn't matter now. Not only does that mean Noah can't have the weekend off, he won't even have Christmas afternoon off like he'd planned."

"Oh, poor Lindsay."

Paul sighed. "Well, maybe you can soften the blow for her. You're still going with the group to Ladybug Farm, right?"

"I am," agreed Derrick unhappily. "But I'm somehow not looking forward to it as much as I once was."

Six hours later Derrick returned with a report that lived up to his expectations.

"Oh, the class was fine," he said, "despite the fact that Bridget almost mixed up the sugar with the salt and preheated the oven to 530 degrees instead of 350."

Paul raised an eyebrow. "That doesn't sound like Bridget."

Derrick had found Paul in the workroom, snipping red and white carnations for the dinner table centerpieces. Derrick began adding a sprig of evergreen to each of the silver bud vases on the work counter while Paul handed him either a red or a white carnation. "She received bad news,

I'm afraid," Derrick explained. "Her grand-daughter has an ear infection and can't fly, so of course that means no one can come for Christmas. Literally, no one. The ladies will be all alone for Christmas."

"Not all alone," Paul objected. "They'll have us."

Derrick said, "It's not the same."

Paul sighed. "No, it's not."

"I just thank heavens for the free wine tasting before the cooking class. The place was like a morgue, but all our guests were so lit no one noticed. And the chocolate-peppermint tarts were sublime. Even those awful teenagers managed to follow instructions long enough to create something edible." He placed the last carnation and then frowned. "Aren't we missing a vase? Why are there only six centerpieces?"

Paul muffled a groan of frustration. "Purline polished the vases today. She must have mis-placed one. I don't have time to look for it now. We'll just have to use one crystal vase."

"We can't have just one," Derrick objected. "We either have to do a complete mismatch, or none at all."

Paul gave him a long look, then started plucking flowers and greenery out of the vases. "Very well. Four silver and three crystal."

Derrick went to the cabinet to retrieve the crystal bud vases. "The thing I feel so badly about is that I think Bridget might have gone to her daughter's house in Chicago for Christmas if we hadn't asked her to do the cooking class today," he said.

"And Lindsay might have gone to California with Dominic if we hadn't scheduled the winery tour for our group," Paul agreed.

"Of course, that would have left Cici all alone," said Derrick, lining up the vases on the counter again.

Paul put down the evergreen sprig he had been about to arrange, a slow speculative light beginning to grow in his eye. "Not," he said, "if someone surprised her with a trip to Cabo to be with her daughter."

Derrick looked at him, a delighted grin spreading over his face. "And if we could get Lindsay to California . . ."

"And Bridget to Chicago . . ."

"Now *that*'s the kind of Christmas money can't buy!" declared Derrick, clapping his hands together in excitement.

"Actually," Paul reminded him, "it's going to cost a good deal of money."

"But it's for the girls!" Derrick said. "The sky's the limit."

"Precisely," said Paul, taking out his phone.

"But it's almost Christmas Eve," Derrick worried. "Is it even possible?"

"All things are possible to good men of good

intention," Paul sang out happily and raised his phone to his ear. With his other hand he made busy typing motions. "Go! Get on the computer, work your phone. We have three flights to catch!"

December 24

Happy Christmas Eve! We have a gala day of old-fashioned Christmas festivity planned for you, so relax and let us do the work. If you haven't quite finished your shopping yet, or just want to pick up a little something special for that someone special, the Hummingbird House van will be making an excursion into the charming town of Staunton today, where you're sure to find a selection of unusual gifts for those on your list. Just a reminder: we have order forms for Ladybug Farm wine at the front desk. Leave your order with us and your wine will be delivered to your front door when you return home. And remember, transportation to and from Christmas Eve religious services at nearby churches, including midnight mass, can be arranged by request.

Your hosts,
Paul and Derrick

6:00–10:00 a.m.	Coffee and pastries available in the dining room
8:30 a.m.	Country breakfast is served in the dining room

10:30 a.m.	Shuttle departs for shopping excursion in Staunton
1:00 p.m.	A light buffet lunch will be available in the dining room for those who remain
3:00 p.m.	Shuttle returns from shopping excursion
4:00 p.m.	A Christmas Eve High Tea is served in the front parlor
6:00–	
8:00 p.m.	Cocktails available in the garden, including mulled wine and amaretto hot chocolate
8:00 p.m.	Informal fondue supper by the fire in the front parlor, accompanied by the Shenandoah Chamber Group

FOURTEEN

Christmas Presents

The Christmas tree in the Magnolia Suite was decorated with silk magnolia blossoms, white and silver glass spheres, and miniature white lights. It was arranged before a window with a white satin tree skirt—embellished with felt magnolia blossoms, naturally—but there were no presents under the tree. If they had been at home their tree would have been piled so high with gifts by now that the packages would have taken up half the room. One year it had taken most of the day simply to open the gifts. The closer it got to Christmas, the more pathetic this whole family vacation got.

Pamela poked her head in from the adjoining room to find her dad sorting through the drawers in the nightstand with a distracted frown on his face. "Hey, Dad," she said. "Mom said it was okay for me to take that shuttle to town today if it was okay with you."

"Hmm?" He glanced at her absently. "Okay. Sure." He went over to a walnut highboy and opened a drawer, searching through it. "Other adults are going too, right?"

"I guess. She also said I could use your credit card."

He closed the drawer, still frowning a little, and reached for his wallet on top of the dresser. "Sure," he said.

"That's okay." She held up the card between her thumb and forefinger. "I already got it."

"Okay. Have a good time." He went to the closet and took out his suitcase, searching inside the pockets.

Pamela hesitated. "Did you lose something, Dad?"

He murmured, "I don't see how I could have."

She shrugged. "Okay, see you later."

She grabbed her coat from the pile of clothes and other miscellany on her bed and pulled it on as she went out into the hallway. Kelly came up behind her. "Where're you going?"

"Christmas shopping."

"For a new phone?"

"So what if I am?"

"I'm telling."

Pamela walked faster. "I don't care."

"Anyway, Mom didn't say you could go." Kelly quickened her step to keep up.

"Yes she did."

"I heard her tell you right before she left with her car keys this morning to stay here and stop pestering."

Pamela shrugged, stuffing her hands in her pockets. "She changed her mind."

"No, she didn't. She got in the car and drove off."

"Probably to buy me a new phone."

"I don't think so. She looked mad to me."

Pamela spun around so abruptly that Kelly almost bumped into her. "What do you want?"

"I'm coming too."

"No you're not! I'm not having some little kid tagging around with me all day."

"Then I'm telling."

Kelly turned around to march back down the hall and Pam called after her, "Go ahead! See if I—"

There was a crash from behind the door of the room opposite them, followed by a string of muffled curses. The door, which had a wreath on it decorated with green velvet ribbons and emerald Christmas ornaments, was partially open. From behind it they heard Mrs. Hildebrand call, "Well, don't just stand there, you worthless girls! Come in and give me a hand."

Pamela hesitated, then went to the door, Kelly close behind her. Pamela gave her sister a disparaging look and pushed the door open wider. "Hey, are you talking to us?" she said, and then stopped, horrified and staring. "Oh my God," she whispered.

Kelly, peering over her shoulder, clapped a hand over her mouth with a muffled squeal of revulsion. "Oh my God!"

Mathilda Hildebrand eyed them both from the floor, her expression dry and resigned. She said wearily, "Oh, my God."

• • •

Paul said, "No, it's true! Why would we tease you about a thing like this?"

"It was a miracle, really," Derrick put in. "And we're terribly sorry for the short notice, but who would have guessed we could find three tickets on Christmas Eve for flights out of our own local airport? Of course, there are a few connections . . ."

"But you are absolutely guaranteed to be in Mexico by midnight, Cici," Paul said, "and Lindsay, you'll be in Sacramento by nine, Bridget in Chicago before the little ones climb into their jammies tonight." They were on speakerphone, and the squeals and chatter of the three women on the other end almost drowned out the two men's voices. Paul tried to make his tone sound serious as he added, "But only if you want to, of course. We understand it's all very last minute."

"Of *course* we want to!" Cici's screech of delight made Paul wince through his smile and cover one ear—only one, because he wanted to hear what the others were saying.

"Are you kidding?" cried Bridget. "Are you seriously kidding me?"

And Lindsay exclaimed, "I'm calling Dominic right now! No—I'm not going to call him at all, I'm going to surprise him! I can't wait to see the look on his face! No, I'd better call, otherwise how will he know to pick me up at the airport?

Oh, I could just kiss you both! How can we ever repay you?"

Paul was grinning so broadly his face hurt, and the look on Derrick's face reflected his own. There had never been a better Christmas gift, for either of them, than hearing the excitement in their friends' voices.

Derrick leaned toward the speaker. "No time for kisses, darlings, or phone calls either. Our man Mick will be by for you in an hour. He'll have your boarding passes all printed out and ready to go. So just fling a few things in a bag and don't forget your toothbrushes."

"And don't worry about Ida Mae," Paul added. "We'll make sure she gets to church in the morning and then we'll bring her back over here for Christmas."

"And," added Derrick, "we'll have our man take care of feeding the animals and whatnot while you're away. So just enjoy yourselves."

"Oh my." Bridget's voice sounded teary. "You've thought of everything! I just don't know what to say."

"Merry Christmas, my dears!" Paul sang out.

And Derrick added, "Bon Voyage!"

When the flurry of laughter and thank-yous and kissy sounds was over and the speakerphone was quiet, Paul and Derrick sank back again into their individual chairs on either side of the big desk and beamed at each other. "Do you know," observed Derrick contentedly, "Purline was right. It's far more blessed to give than to receive."

Paul lifted an eyebrow. "Did Purline say that?"

"I'm fairly certain."

"Well," allowed Paul, "whoever said it had a point. I can't remember a more delightful Christmas, can you?"

"The best gift I ever got was the one I gave away," observed Derrick in happy agreement.

"Did Purline say that too?"

Derrick just smiled. "No, I did."

"Well in that case," replied Paul, "Amen."

Pamela said, staring at the abomination on the floor beside Mrs. Hildebrand's bed, "You have an artificial leg."

The older woman replied sharply, "In fact, I have several, not that any of them are doing me any good at the moment."

Kelly said, big-eyed, "Ew, gross."

Mrs. Hildebrand extended a demanding hand to them from her position on the floor. "Are you going to help me up, or are you just going to stand there?"

It was at that moment that a man's voice said behind them, "Mrs. Hildebrand, are you all right?"

"Clearly I am not!" she retorted, and Mick moved past the girls and into the room.

The teenagers stared at his attire, but said nothing as he helped the older woman to the reading chair beside the fireplace. The older woman also looked him over from head to toe, and demanded as she settled into the chair, "What are you supposed to be?"

He smiled. "The same thing I've always been. Are you hurt? Can I get you anything?"

"You may not," she informed him imperiously. "You . . ." She pointed to Kelly. "May bring me my walking stick. And you . . ." She turned her pointing finger on Pamela. "Bring me my prosthesis."

Pamela walked hesitantly over to the bed and, with a look on her face that was somewhere between fascination and disgust, she gingerly picked up the artificial limb and took it to its owner. Kelly crept over to Mrs. Hildebrand's chair with the bejeweled walking stick and just stood there, looking as though she expected the woman to grow a pair of black, leathery wings and fly away.

Pamela said timidly, "How, um . . . what happened? To your leg, I mean?"

"None of your damn business." She glared at Mick. "Well, you don't expect me to hike up my skirt with you standing there, do you? Go on about your business."

He gave her a small bow. "Mrs. Hildebrand, it's always a pleasure."

He turned to go, but she stopped him with a sharp, "Wait." When he turned back to her she regarded him with narrowed eyes, but when she spoke there was, for the first time, the faintest trace of raw emotion in her voice, perhaps even a hint of vulnerability. "Tell me the truth. Why are you here? Is it for me?"

He assured her gently, "No. Not this time." And then he winked. "Actually, it might surprise you to know that you're here for me."

She scowled to cover her relief. "Doesn't surprise me a bit," she returned gruffly. "I always pay my debts."

Kelly looked from one to the other of them with interest. "Do you guys know each other?"

Mrs. Hildebrand told her shortly, "Mind your own business."

Mick's eyes twinkled as he said, "See you later, Mrs. Hildebrand."

"A good deal later, I hope," she retorted.

He chuckled and turned for the door, then glanced back at Pamela. "Ask her about the Haiti earthquake," he suggested. "You'll be the first to ever get the full story out of her." He gave Mrs. Hildebrand another small bow and added, "Again, it's been a pleasure. If I don't see you before then, Merry Christmas."

Both girls looked as though they wanted to follow him out the door, but then Pamela hesitated, looking back at Mrs. Hildebrand. "You were in an earthquake?" she said.

FIFTEEN

We Wish You a Merry Christmas

The Hummingbird House van was rollicking with the excited chatter and laughter of the three women in the middle seat. "I forgot sunscreen," said Cici. "Do you think they'll have sunscreen at the hotel?"

"In Mexico? Probably. As long as you didn't forget your passport."

"Wait! Wait—oh, never mind, it's okay, there it is."

"I can't believe we're doing this!" declared Bridget. She was practically bouncing with excitement. "Running away from home on Christmas Eve! Who *does* that?"

"People who are a lot younger than us, I'll tell you that. I don't think I packed any underwear."

"Did you reach your daughter in Chicago?" Lindsay asked Bridget. "I can't get a signal on my phone."

"I had to leave a message. They're probably out doing some last-minute shopping. Oh my goodness, I can't believe we're doing this!" Then, "Oh, no. I forgot gloves. It's ten degrees in Chicago!"

"Maybe someone will give you some for Christmas," said Cici.

Lindsay dug into her coat pocket. "Here, take mine. I'm going to California! But it certainly would be nice if my husband was waiting for me at the airport. Cici, let me see your phone."

"Nothing," said Cici, but passed the phone to her anyway. "I'll wait 'til I get to the airport to call Lori. The one thing I don't want to do is walk in on their honeymoon, even if it *is* Christmas!"

"They're going to be thrilled to see you," Bridget assured her.

"Who cares if they are or not?" replied Cici happily. "I'm going to Cabo!"

Lindsay returned the phone to Cici and turned to look at the couple in the backseat. "Excuse me. Can either of you get a signal?"

Geoffery Windsor took out his phone and glanced at it. "I'm afraid not."

Angela Phipps, sitting next to him, slipped her phone out of the oversized bag on the seat next to her, looked at it and shook her head. "We must be in one of those dead zones."

Lindsay sighed. "This whole valley is a dead zone. The Hummingbird House is the only place for miles that even *has* cell service, and I've never understood how that happened." She leaned forward and tapped one of the teenagers on the shoulder. "Excuse me, hi. I don't suppose either of you have a working phone, do you?"

Geoffery smiled politely, if distantly, at Angela as she returned her phone to her bag. She had joined the excursion at the last minute, which had surprised Geoffery because neither she nor her husband had done more than go through the motions of being social since they arrived. "Your husband is not much of a shopper, huh?"

"What?" She looked blank for a moment, then recovered herself with a vague smile. "Oh, no, he much prefers a fireplace and a good book."

"I'm surprised no more people took advantage of the chance to go to town this afternoon," he added in a moment, just to have something to say.

"I believe two of the couples went to tour the caverns. The Mathesons and the Canons."

He nodded and smiled, and turned his gaze out the window so that she wouldn't feel compelled to continue a conversation in which she clearly wasn't interested. The ladies in the seat in front of them continued to chatter away excitedly while bare branches and brown frozen fields sailed by alongside the lonely country road on which they traveled.

In a moment Angela Phipps surprised him by saying, "You're leaving us then, Mr. Windsor?"

He glanced at her, and she indicated the leather overnight bag at his feet. He said, trying to make it all sound easy and predetermined, "It was generous of our hosts to ask me to stay the whole weekend, but I really just came to do the reading. I'd like to be home for Christmas." Home had not existed since Liz died, and the one-bedroom apartment where he now lived held so little appeal that he often found he couldn't remember what it looked like after he'd been away for a few days.

She turned and looked out the window herself for a time. Then she said, "My father used to love shopping on Christmas Eve. All the crowds and the lights and the madness. It was kind of a tradition with him."

Geoffery pretended a polite interest. "So you're keeping up the tradition?"

"No," she replied flatly. She did not even look away from the window. "I don't do that anymore."

There really wasn't a reply to that. Still, Geoffery might have said something to break the awkwardness that followed. But just then there was a grinding sound from the engine, a soft *bang,* and, with cries of alarm from many of its passengers, the van lurched and clattered to a stop.

"Did you hear Mr. Windsor decided to leave after all?" Derrick said, coming into the parlor where Paul was setting up for tea. He had a basket filled with white Irish linen tablecloths and napkins that were embroidered with tiny roses along the hemline—very Christmassy—as well as fresh candles to replace the ones they had burned yesterday. Paul had already freshened the flowers, laid the fire, and brought the three-tiered pastry servers out of the pantry. The Christmas Eve tea would not be served for another five hours, but the key to effortless hosting was advance preparation.

"I did," Paul said. He rolled a tea cart into position, its wheels clattering on the wood floors.

"A pity." Derrick snapped open a tablecloth and draped it over one of the round occasional tables that were drawn up near the fireplace. "I think he would have enjoyed the concert tomorrow, and of course that completely throws off our seating arrangement for Christmas dinner." He placed one of the serving tiers in the middle of the table, flanked by two sprigs of holly arranged just so.

"Ah well, Christmas is for family, I suppose." Paul gave the tier a half-turn, observed it critically, and adjusted one of the holly sprigs.

Derrick thrust a handful of napkins at him. "Well, if you ask me . . ."

"Did you all see this?" Purline came into the parlor, rustling a newspaper purposefully. "Take a look at it. Just look!"

She thrust the newspaper at Paul and thumped one of the articles with a thumb and forefinger. "It's all right there in black and white. Just read it for yourself!" She took a step back and waited with hands on jeaned hips, her expression a mixture of eager anticipation and grim satisfaction. "And don't be saying I didn't tell you so, either!"

Derrick came to read over Paul's shoulder, and Paul glanced uncertainly at Purline before he read, "Police Seek Man in String of Robberies." He glanced again at Purline and went on, "'Evanson police are looking for a man in connection with several burglaries that have occurred there in the past two weeks.'" He stopped and looked at Purline. "Purline, this is in the next county. What . . ."

"Go on," she insisted, nodding her head vigorously.

With a resigned breath, he turned back to the article. "The suspect is described as six feet three inches tall, two hundred forty pounds, with dark hair and beard. He was last seen wearing a black leather jacket and leather motorcycle boots. The suspect is said to have . . ." Again he stopped, but did not look up. "To have a Hell's Angel insignia tattooed on his arm."

Derrick snatched the paper from him to read it for himself. "Oh good heavens."

"This doesn't mean anything," Paul said impatiently. "Our Mick doesn't even have a beard."

Derrick cheered. "That's right, he doesn't!"

"Are you telling me them whiskers he wears down to his neck don't look like a beard to you?" Purline challenged. "It's him, I'm telling you." She thumped the paper again. "You go on and read about it—he stole a computer from one lady's house while she was sleeping in the room next door! Wiped out another family's whole Christmas, got everything under the tree! Then went back for the TV set! And you said yourself, a lot of stuff has gone missing around here since he showed up."

Paul frowned. "Like my crepe pans."

"Oh, will you get over your blessed crepe pans? I told you, you packed them in some Christmas box somewhere. I'm talking about valuable stuff!"

"Like my letter opener," Derrick said uneasily.

"And that silver flower vase you said was in the pantry that nobody ever found, not to mention your fancy candlesticks."

"We have a lot of candlesticks, Purline," Paul said, but even he was sounding less than confident now. "It's entirely possible they were misplaced."

"Besides," Derrick insisted, trying to summon conviction, "it doesn't even make sense. We have art on the walls worth thousands, valuable antiques and electronics in every room. What kind of thief takes a candlestick and leaves an iPad?"

"A smart one," returned Purline. "You can pawn silver anywhere, and it's a lot easier to sneak out of the house than a computer. You do what you want to, but if it was me, I'd be on the phone to the sheriff's office right now."

Paul looked at Derrick uncomfortably. "It might

not be such a terrible idea to ask them to run a background check."

"On Christmas Eve?" Derrick objected. "After all Mick's done for us? I'd be mortified."

Purline rolled her eyes. "Well, just don't say I didn't warn you. I'll be setting out lunch in twenty minutes, then I've got to scoot and pick up the kids so's my husband Bill can get over to the church to help set up the nativity scene for the singing tonight. They're having a real donkey and everything. Y'all ought to come by if you get a chance. Don't worry, though, I'll be back before the hour's up to clear the tables and get your fondue pots mixed up."

Paul murmured absently, "Thank you, Purline."

"You're a treasure," added Derrick, still looking at the paper.

She gave them both a meaningful nod. "Sheriff's telephone number is nine-one-one."

SIXTEEN

Christmas Stories

No worries, folks," Mick had said cheerfully just before he got out of the van. "I'll have her back on her feet in no time."

That had been before he lifted the hood and a plume of smoke billowed out, before he returned for the third time to assure them everything was under control, before Lindsay and Cici had hiked half a mile in opposite directions trying to get a cell phone signal, and before what must have been the fifth car zoomed by them on the narrow country road without stopping, slowing down, or even glancing in their direction.

"I don't understand why no one stops," Bridget said, twisting her head to follow the wake of the latest vehicle that had left them behind. "It's Christmas Eve, for heaven's sake."

Geoffery, sitting behind her, did not want to point out that if he had come across a broken down van attended by a tattooed man in a too-small tuxedo, motorcycle boots and a Frosty-the-Snowman skullcap, he wouldn't have stopped either. Instead he offered, "I'm sure one of them will report a stranded vehicle. People do, you know, even when they don't stop."

Bridget turned in her seat and smiled hesitantly. "Mr. Windsor, I'm sure you hear this all the time, but I loved your book. It helped me get through a very difficult time. I was hoping to see you yesterday at the cooking class, but I'm glad I got to tell you that."

Geoffery hesitated, putting the pieces together. "Oh," he said. "Ms. Tindale. Right, the cooking class. Sorry I missed it."

She said, continuing to smile, "You're leaving us, then? I'm on my way to see my daughter and grandchildren, too. It'll be the first time in three years! There's nothing like family at Christmas, is there?"

He replied, without exactly knowing why, "Actually, my wife is dead. I don't have a family."

He saw the familiar confusion and sympathy cross her face. "I'm so sorry," she said. "How awful to be alone at Christmas."

He sensed, rather than saw, Angela's gaze turn toward him. And he said, quietly and as kindly as he could, "Actually, sometimes it's worse to be with people."

Bridget's smile faltered. "Oh," she said. "Well. Maybe someone will call for help, like you said." She turned to face forward again.

Cici slid open the van door in time to hear that and said, "Well, if they do it won't be for a while."

"Still no signal?" said Bridget, dismayed.

Cici shook her head as she climbed inside.

"And the houses are so far apart here I'd rather not try to walk to one."

"This is so lame," said one of the girls in the first row. "How can this be so lame?"

Her sister replied, "In the lamest place ever? You've got to be kidding me."

Lindsay opened the other sliding door and climbed inside. "No luck," she reported, and the heads that had turned hopefully toward her looked away again. "And," she added in a slightly lower tone, "not that I'm one to judge, but I don't think our driver knows anything at all about car engines."

Cici muffled a groan. "Great. My flight leaves in an hour and a half. Even if we got on the road right now I'd barely make it."

Lindsay said, "I'm sure none of the flights will leave on time today." But she sounded worried too.

Geoffery glanced at his seat companion, who was resting her head against the windowpane with an expression of complete disinterest on her face. He said, "Maybe I'd better see if there's anything I can do to help."

He did not know any more about cars than anyone else in the vehicle, but spirits were starting to sink inside the van and he could use the fresh air. Besides, there was still something about his last conversation with that man Mick that made him uneasy, and he would feel better keeping an eye on him.

He walked to the front of the van, where Mick had spread a drop cloth over the engine and lined up what appeared to be the contents of the vehicle's emergency repair kit on top. Mick himself was bent intently over the engine with a wrench in hand, and he looked up with a grin when Geoffery walked up.

"How's it going?"

"No worries," he replied cheerfully, "right on schedule."

Geoffery glanced at his watch. "The other passengers are getting a little concerned they're going to miss their flights. And no one can get a cell phone signal."

"Doesn't surprise me a bit." Mick turned back to his work.

"We've been here over an hour."

"Everyone has somewhere important to be for Christmas." And then he glanced up at Geoffery with a smile. "Except yourself, of course. You just need to be wherever you're not."

Geoffery was silent for a moment. Then he said evenly, "You don't have the first idea what you're doing with that engine, do you?"

Mick just winked and starting banging around with the wrench again.

The van door opened and the two teenagers climbed out, sniping at each other about something Geoffery didn't hear and didn't want to. They stalked away into the weeds on the side of the road, one of them holding her phone up to the sky as though expecting the gods of technology to strike it with life-giving lightning. In a moment, Angela Phipps climbed out of the van and walked around to the front.

"Excuse me," she said. "I know you're doing the best you can, but I wonder if you could give me an idea how much longer it will be? I'm flying standby and the last flight tonight leaves at six."

Geoffery looked at her in surprise.

Mick replied pleasantly, "Don't you worry, ma'am. I'll get you where you need to be."

The door opened again and the other three women climbed out. Angela turned to them with a helpless shrug and walked a few feet away to stand in the sun, hands in the pockets of her coat.

Cici said worriedly, "Maybe we *should* start walking."

Bridget looked in dismay at her high-heeled boots. "In these?"

"Anyway," Lindsay said, "who knows how far we'd have to go before we got a signal, or found a house where someone was home? Let's wait a while longer."

"We don't want to wait too long," Cici said. "It starts getting dark early this time of year."

They all glanced at one another uneasily. The possibility of being stranded overnight had not previously occurred to them.

Lindsay said, "Remember that Christmas we

waited all day for Noah? I was sick with worry."

"He walked four hours to get home," Bridget said with an affectionate shake of her head. "Crazy kid."

Lindsay smiled with remembrance and explained to Geoffery and Angela, "Noah's my son."

"We all claim him," Cici put in.

"He's in the military now," Bridget added. "We thought he might be able to come home for Christmas, but his leave was canceled at the last minute."

Angela made a sympathetic sound, but it was clear she wasn't interested in conversation. They all stood together awkwardly beside the van for a while, listening, with slowly diminishing hope, to the clanging sounds coming from the front.

The teenagers returned, stomping and kicking through the dead grass like young colts with a grudge. The oldest one, Pamela, went up to Mick and demanded, "So how long do the stores in this place stay open, anyway?"

He glanced up with a smile. "Sorry, young lady, I'm not from around here. Afraid I couldn't guess."

Cici volunteered, "I'm sure quite a few will be open late on Christmas Eve."

Lindsay added, "It depends on what kind of store you're looking for, I imagine. There are a lot of cute shops in Staunton, but it's usually the boutiques that close early."

Kelly, the youngest one, said, "What about toy stores?"

Bridget looked amused, and so, briefly, did the other women. "Aren't you girls a little old for toys?"

Pamela scowled. "It's not for us," she muttered. She stalked away and sat down hard on a patch of dead grass beside the van, drawing her knees up to her chin.

Kelly looked at Mick boldly. "We did what you said," she said. "We asked her about the earthquake."

Mick glanced up from his work with lifted eyebrow. "Did you, now?"

"Of course we didn't believe her," Kelly said. "What kind of lame-brain believes everything an old woman says? So we looked it up on my iPad. It was true, every word. Turns out she really does know Bono, too. There were pictures."

"Good for you," Geoffery murmured, and looked away.

Lindsay said curiously, "What earthquake?"

Kelly turned to her, straightening her shoulders with her own sense of importance. "The one in Haiti. I guess it was a pretty big deal. A lot of people died and stuff. She was there, the old woman—Mrs. Hildebrand, I mean—supervising a photo shoot for her magazine. She was really old then too, I guess, but she went anyway. Anyway, the earthquake happened, and she tried to take cover in the doorway of this building, only it fell down. The whole building."

Geoffery turned to her, listening, and so did everyone else. Mick stopped banging the wrench, and Angela straightened up to look at the girl.

Kelly went on, "There were a lot of kids inside. Turns out it was an orphanage. They were all hurt and scared, and Mrs. Hildebrand, she was trapped under this big steel beam . . ."

"Post," corrected Pamela without looking around. "It was a post that held up a wall, and it was concrete not steel."

Kelly shrugged. "Anyway, she was trapped so she couldn't help the kids. They were there for a long time . . ."

"Three days," said Pamela, and everyone looked at her. "They were there for three days."

"Oh my God," Bridget said softly.

"And it was hot and dark, and the kids were hungry and thirsty and thinking probably no one would ever find them, but you know what she did? Mrs. Hildebrand, that is. She told them stories to keep their spirits up. For three days she told them stories."

"Like Scheherazade," put in Pamela.

"We looked that up, too," Kelly said. "So anyway, eventually the firemen or whatever found them, but they had to cut off Mrs. Hildebrand's leg to get her out. Now she has an artificial leg."

"Lots of them," corrected Pamela. "One for each pair of shoes."

The attention of the adults was riveted on the two girls. Angela whispered, "How awful."

Geoffery murmured, "I never knew that."

Pam pushed herself to her feet. "There were fifteen of them," she said. "Fifteen that got out alive, at least. Mrs. Hildebrand helped rebuild the orphanage, and most of those same kids are still there. She goes to see them a couple of times a year. She said she was going down there next month and . . ." She added with a defiant lift of her chin, "They're not too old for toys."

"We know she's rich and all," Kelly added, "and probably gives them everything they need. But we thought it would be kind of cool if they got Christmas presents from some American kids. Even though they won't get there for Christmas."

The silence that followed while the gathered adults simply smiled in wonder and tenderness at the two girls seemed to embarrass both of them. Pamela broke it abruptly by turning to Mick. "And it's not going to happen at all, is it," she demanded belligerently, "if you don't get this van started."

Mick ducked his head to hide his smile, and picked up the wrench again.

"I really can't imagine what's keeping the others," Derrick said, fussing anxiously with the tea service. "I'm sure they'll be here at any minute. Mick is very reliable about keeping a schedule."

But even as he spoke what he only hoped was not a lie, Paul appeared at the door of the parlor with his phone in hand and a distressed look on his face. Mick did not have a cell phone—which they realized only now was a mistake on their parts—and attempts to reach Cici, Lindsay or Bridget for a progress report had so far failed. That meant nothing, of course, as they were probably all in the air by now. But from the anxiety in Paul's eyes as he beckoned to Derrick, there must have been news, and it could not be good.

"They might have run into traffic," suggested Adele, placing a festively decorated finger sandwich on her plate, and then, throwing caution to the wind, another.

"Oh, sweetie," objected her sister Sheila, "those may be small, but you know they're nothing but calorie bombs. I'll have another, too, if you don't mind."

After a morning of sightseeing, the two couples had returned full of their usual high spirits, anxious to chat about all they'd seen. Mrs. Hildebrand, the only other attendee at the elaborate Christmas Eve tea, had seemed less than enthused by their adventures, and had taken her teacup over to the window. There she stood and gazed out at the garden, sipping silently, and left the four friends to relive their adventures among themselves. Neither Bryce Phipps nor Carl Bartlett had as yet made an appearance.

Derrick said, in as easy a tone as possible, "Enjoy, everyone. I'll be right back. Mrs. Hildebrand," he added as he passed her, "did I mention how lovely you look this afternoon? That color of blue really brings out your eyes."

She gave him a skeptical look for his trouble, and he didn't linger.

Paul clutched Derrick's arm and pulled him out into the hallway the minute he was within reach. "What?" Derrick demanded in an urgent stage whisper. "What did you hear? It wasn't from the hospital, was it? There hasn't been an accident?"

Paul shook his head adamantly, but there were pinched white lines around his lips and his eyes were dark with despair. "No, no, I haven't been able to reach anyone. But Derrick . . ." His fingers tightened on Derrick's arm. "It's gone!"

Derrick stared at him, baffled. "What's gone?"

Wordlessly, Paul pulled him down the hall into the reception room, where Purline stood beside the desk with her arms crossed and a grim expression on her face. Paul flung out a dramatic hand toward the desk and cried, "Look!"

At first Derrick didn't understand. He scanned all the walls to make sure the artwork was in place, and then his eyes fell on the tall reception desk with its fluffy cotton batting display and . . .

"The train!" he gasped, staring. "Where is it?"

"Well, if I knew that, would I have bothered you?" Paul retorted sharply. Then he ran a hand over his face distractedly. "I thought perhaps Purline had moved it . . ."

"Although why in the world he would think that I don't know," interrupted Purline smartly. "It's not like I haven't been told a hundred times not to dust the collectibles."

"Or maybe she'd seen someone come in . . ."

"Like that could never happen," Purline interrupted again, "since you never lock the front door, and with people coming in and out every minute. I told you and told you to put a bell on that door, but do you listen to me? Who hasn't been in and out of here this morning, that's what I'd like to know. First that woman in the magnolia room goes tearing out of here like a house a'fire, then those people going to the caverns, then that doctor fella, then the UPS man left a bunch of packages in here—don't you worry, I put them all in the rooms they were for—but you know the only person that matters was that Mick fella you all are so wild about, and he musta been in and out of here a half dozen times before he got everybody loaded up and out of here."

"It's been in my family for generations," Paul said, but it came out as more of a groan. "It's worth . . ."

"Six thousand, five hundred dollars," Derrick

murmured, and then he explained, "at least that's what the nearest facsimile went for at auction several years ago. But how could Mick—I mean, anyone—know that?"

Purline sniffed. "Are you kidding?" She jerked her head at Paul. "He talks about that train almost as much as he whines about them crepe pans. Everybody in this place knows what it's worth."

Paul looked stricken. "I do, don't I?" He sank back heavily against the desk. "It's my fault," he said weakly. "I was boastful and careless and now it's gone. Stolen right out from under my nose. How could I be so foolish?"

Derrick said, "There's got to be an explanation."

"You know what the explanation is as well as I do," said Purline, "and it's driving down the road right now with your friends and your paying customers and all your valuables!"

Then, at the look of genuine alarm that came into both men's faces, she softened her tone. "I'm real sorry this happened to you," she said, "and I'm sure everybody's okay—I mean, I hope they are—but if you don't call the sheriff . . ."

"Excuse me, Mr. Slater, Mr. Anderson." Carl Bartlett came from the corridor where his room was located, looking worried and unsure. "I don't mean to bother you, but my girls went on the shopping excursion this morning and I expected them back by now. I wonder if you've heard anything?"

Paul and Derrick looked at each other uncertainly while Purline held them both in her steely gaze. Then Derrick said, with as much heartiness as he could possibly muster, "Just a slight delay, Mr. Bartlett, it's Christmas Eve, after all. I'm sure they'll be here any moment. In the meantime, why don't you go enjoy tea with the others?"

Derrick lifted an arm to turn him toward the parlor, but the other man didn't seem to notice. His worried frown only deepened. "It's just that I didn't want to say anything until I talked to them, and my wife's phone seems to be off . . . I don't like to raise the alarm for nothing, but I really don't know what could have happened . . ."

He sighed, and seemed to come to a decision. "You see, I brought the Christmas gifts I'd intended to give my wife and daughters with me here. They were rather valuable, I'm afraid— jewelry. They've been locked in my suitcase all this time because I didn't want the girls to find them and ruin the surprise. But when I went to get them out this morning to put them under the tree, the lock on my suitcase was broken and the gifts were gone. I've searched every inch of the suite. I just don't know what could have happened."

Paul and Derrick looked at Purline in despair. She said, "Now?"

Paul gave a great and sorrowful sigh. "Now," he agreed.

• • •

The sun slanted in the sky, warming the ground where they stood but bringing the promise of a crisp cold night in the breeze it left behind. There were a few false starts as the engine almost, but inevitably failed, to catch, and each one seemed a little less disappointing than the last. Bridget broke out a Tupperware container of cookies she had packed for her grandchildren, and Lindsay found a package of cheese crackers she had tucked into her purse for the trip and added them to the feast. Cici found a six-pack of water in the console of the van. One of the teenagers passed around a pack of gum. Their little group grew comfortable together, more like friends at a casual party than strangers stranded on the road.

Geoffery wished he had gone to the cooking class and gotten to know the women of Ladybug Farm. He wished he'd made more of an effort with Mrs. Hildebrand. He wondered about the people back at the Hummingbird House, all of whom he had missed the chance to know. Geoffery turned to Angela and said, "I didn't know you were leaving."

There was a slight hesitance, and then she replied, pleasantly enough, "I hadn't planned to, but when I heard the van was stopping at the airport on the way to town it seemed foolish not to take the opportunity."

He waited for her to continue, but when she

didn't, the journalist in him wouldn't let it drop. He said, "Your husband . . . ?"

She replied without looking at him, "I thought it was best that I make this trip alone." Then she seemed to surprise herself by adding, in a perfectly normal tone, "We're divorcing."

One of the ladies, overhearing, gasped softly and all of them looked at her in concern. Bridget said with genuine sympathy, "Oh dear. I'm sorry. That's terrible news at Christmas. It must be very upsetting for you."

Angela released a tired breath. "Not really. It's been a long time coming. Thirty-five years, to be exact."

Geoffery wished he had never inquired. He was not comfortable being trapped inside the details of someone else's life. He cast about for something to say, but all he could come up with was, "It's a little chilly out here." It wasn't really, and the sun felt nice. "Maybe we should wait inside the van."

No one made a move to do so. Lindsay said gently, "I know it's none of my business, but you've been together so long . . . surely there's a way to work this out."

Angela just smiled and shook her head. "Thank you for your concern. But it's misplaced."

Bridget had never been one to simply let a matter go. She said, "You both seemed so happy together yesterday at the cooking class. Your husband is—seemed to be—such a nice man."

Angela leaned against the van and gazed into the distance, her eyes squinted a little against the sun. "We've both had a lot of practice looking happy together. It's an art form really. Which isn't to say that Bryce isn't a perfectly nice man, because he is. This isn't his fault. I wouldn't want anyone to think that. If anything, he tried harder than I did. I mean, he established a whole foundation, for God's sake. He had a trauma center named after him. He tried to make it all count for something. But in the end it all boiled down to the fact that we couldn't forgive each other." She turned pale, quiet eyes on Bridget and said, "We couldn't forgive each other for killing our son."

There was a collective held breath. Bridget's fingertips fluttered to her lips but no one else moved. Geoffery thought, *I don't want to know this; this has nothing to do with me; I don't want to be inside this nice woman's life, I don't want to see behind the curtain. I don't even know her, I don't know any of these people. I've got my own problems. Leave me out of this.*

But in the end he was the one who said quietly, "What happened?"

She answered. He had not expected her to, but she did. Her voice was flat and expressionless, almost a monotone, but she answered. "We were young and ambitious and, dare I say it, privileged.

The golden children from golden families. Bryce was already on a career track for chief surgeon, and I was doing monthly features in two magazines and had offers for others. I was into interior design back then. Still, we both knew that David was the most perfect thing either one of us would ever create. We loved him intensely, madly, to the exclusion of all else. It was as though he was the reason we existed, not the other way around." She smiled then, but it seemed like an autonomic function, a simple curve of the lips unprompted by intention or emotion. And it faded almost before it was fully formed.

"It was a typical Monday morning," she said, "the week before Christmas. You know how frantic it can be that time of year. I was late for a meeting, Bryce was supposed to be taking David to school. He was six. We'd all been Christmas shopping that weekend, and David couldn't stop chattering about the 'secret' presents he'd gotten for each of us, throwing out so many hints I was sure he was going to give the whole thing away before the end of the day. You know how children that age are. Anyway, I was barely listening, and I was in such a rush I'm not sure I even kissed David good-bye. I got in the car and realized I'd forgotten my portfolio. I ran back in the house to get it, and by that time I figured David was already buckled into Bryce's car. But he wasn't.

Bryce had stopped to take a phone call, and David ran out of the house by himself, and when I started to back out of the driveway . . . I never saw him."

There was a muffled sob, or a catch of breath, from one of the women. Angela did not look around, and nothing about her expression, or her tone, changed. "He lived for thirty-six hours, but he never regained consciousness. Massive head trauma." She took a slow, soft breath. "We don't celebrate Christmas at our house anymore," she said. "We go through the motions—the parties, the fundraisers, the charitable donations. But for the most part, it's just something to be gotten through. Coming here was a mistake. This was all"—she waved her hand vaguely—"a mistake."

Cici said quietly, and with fierce sincerity, "I am so sorry."

Lindsay added, "I never meant to upset you."

Angela seemed to come back to herself with a start, and gave a quick smile and a brief shake of her head. Once again she was the composed, polite and distant woman she had always been. The curtain was closed. "Please, it's I who should apologize. It doesn't upset me to talk about my son. But I'm sorry you had to listen to it. I didn't mean to ruin everyone's holiday."

Geoffery couldn't stop looking at her. He felt as though there was something significant he should say, but he couldn't remember what it was.

So he racked his brain for the few snippets he'd gleaned from his casual conversations with Bryce Phipps, and with others who knew him, over the past several days. He said, "Is that why your husband changed his specialty to neurosurgery? And he established the David Phipps Children's Trauma Center. It's known all over the country."

Angela smiled distantly. "Everyone deals with grief in his own way. My husband found a way to celebrate David's life. I never seem to have been able to get past the moment of his death. And as much as I've always admired Bryce for that," she added slowly, with difficulty, "I think I've also always resented him as well."

"It must be lonely," Lindsay said gently, "for both of you."

Angela looked at her with an odd expression on her face, as though she had never thought of that before. "Yes," she said simply.

Bridget had been strangely quiet, two fingers still lightly covering her lips, her eyes riveted on Angela. Now she said, dropping her hand from her mouth, "My little boy—my Kevin—was hit by a car when he was seven. He was airlifted to George Washington University Hospital in DC. There was a neurosurgeon there giving a lecture, teaching a new technique, I don't know the details. He was supposed to have left already, I remember that much, but his flight was delayed because of fog over Chicago. His name was Dr. Bryce Phipps, and he saved my son's life."

Cici clutched Bridget's arm, her eyes growing bright with tears. "Oh, Bridge," she whispered. "I'd forgotten."

Bridget said, "I never got to thank him." She stepped away from Cici and walked over to Angela, pulling her into a clumsy, heartfelt embrace. Her voice was muffled as she repeated, "I never got to thank him."

Bridget stepped away with tears on her face, but Angela looked simply stunned. Instinctively, Bridget reached up to smooth a strand of errant hair behind Angela's ear, as she might do to a child. "Please don't misunderstand me," she said huskily. "I don't mean to suggest that your son's life was a good trade for mine. What happened was inexplicable, a tragedy beyond measure. But I wanted you to know . . . it had meaning."

Cici stepped in suddenly and embraced Angela. "Kevin married my daughter," she said. "He grew up to marry my daughter and make us all a family."

"It wasn't just one life your husband saved," Lindsay said. "If Kevin had died that night, Bridget would never have been the same. Maybe our friendship wouldn't have survived, maybe we wouldn't have moved to Ladybug Farm, maybe I would never have met Dominic. Maybe none of us would be here now . . ." She gestured helplessly around her. "Where we are today. Everything would have been different."

"Small things change all things," Cici said softly. She looked at Geoffery. "Isn't that what you said in your speech the other day, Mr. Windsor?"

He remembered then what he had wanted to say to Angela. "Yes," Geoffery replied, his eyes on Angela. "I think I did."

Angela glanced at him apologetically. "I'm afraid I haven't read your book."

He smiled. "That's okay. I'm about to start a new one. In the meantime . . ." He took a breath. "Maybe it would be a good thing if you and your husband and I could talk about survivor's guilt." The next words came slowly, from a place deep inside that he'd never really acknowledged before. "I don't think I actually understood what it was until now."

Angela looked around uncertainly, at the strangers who seemed so ready to surround her with love, at the man asking for her goodwill, even at the teenagers sitting nearby and listening so intently. She said, "I . . . I'm not sure . . ."

Suddenly all heads swiveled toward the sound of the cranking engine. Mick leaned out of the open driver's door and beckoned them inside gaily. "All aboard!" he called.

Cici looked at her watch, and the leap of excitement in her eyes died. "Too late," she said.

But then Angela glanced at the two girls, and she smiled, very faintly. "Maybe not," she said.

SEVENTEEN

The Age of Miracles

The smartest thing Derrick had ever done was to break out the champagne before the police arrived. The Mathesons and the Canons were half-buzzed in the parlor, munching on chocolate scones and laughing too loudly as they made plans for next Christmas in Aspen. Mrs. Hildebrand sipped contentedly in the corner, but those bright, birdlike eyes missed nothing as Derrick tried to hurry the sheriff's deputy into the office, where Carl Bartlett waited uneasily with Paul and Purline.

"I don't like to accuse anyone," Bartlett said unhappily, "particularly not without talking to my family. But . . ."

"But it's not just diamonds and emeralds," Purline insisted hotly, "it's a whole bunch of stuff. I started making a list." She thrust the paper into Deputy Richards's hands. "And this is just what I know about."

Deputy Richards glanced at the list. "And you are?"

"Purline Williams. I'm the housekeeper." She craned her neck to see his notebook as he wrote it down. "P-u-r . . ."

"Yes, ma'am, I've got it." He looked at Paul, who was slumped behind the desk, mopping his pasty brow with a handkerchief. "When did you first notice these items were missing?"

"I'm not sure." Then, anxiously, "Is this going to be in the newspaper? We have a stellar reputation here at the Hummingbird House, and if this is in the paper . . ."

"I'll tell you when," interrupted Purline. "When that Hell's Angel first showed up, that's exactly when things started to go missing."

The deputy looked at her alertly. "Hell's Angel?"

She snatched the newspaper from Derrick's desk and thrust it at the officer. "This fellow right here, that's who done it! That same guy that robbed all those poor folks over in Evanston, he's been hanging around here for over a week now and bringing nothing but trouble with him!"

"It's going to be in the paper," Paul moaned. "We're going to be ruined."

Derrick said anxiously to the deputy, "If there's any way you could keep this quiet . . ."

The deputy looked up from the article and said to Purline, "Ma'am, you realize this newspaper is three days old, don't you?"

"Mama." Purline's daughter Naomi stood at the door. "We finished all our chores and we're ready to go now."

Purline glanced at her distractedly. "In a minute, honey. Mama's busy." She looked back at the

248

deputy. "So what if it is? What's what is what, right?"

"Well, yes," he admitted, handing the newspaper back to her. "But this suspect was picked up day before yesterday, and as far as I know he's still in jail. So if we could get a clearer time line . . ."

Purline stared at the newspaper in disbelief. Paul sat up straighter. Derrick cast him a triumphant look. "I *knew* it wasn't him!" Derrick said.

The relief on Paul's face faded slowly to dread. "I just had a horrible thought," he said, turning to Derrick. "Park Sung and Kim Gi. They arrived about the same time as Mick."

Derrick pressed his hand to his heart. "And they don't even speak English," he added ominously.

"And we have no idea what their background is," added Paul.

"We know nothing about them at all except that Harmony sent them," Derrick said.

"Which is hardly an endorsement."

Deputy Richards, tracking the conversation, said, "Could you spell those names for me, please?"

Paul began, "P.A.R. . . ."

Naomi tugged on her mother's sweater. "Mama!"

Purline patted her head absently. "Go get your

stuff together, sweetie, and get your brothers' coats on. Mama will be there in a minute."

Naomi started to run toward the door but then turned back and looked at the two men behind the giant desk. "Mr. Paul and Mr. Derrick, Mama said we mustn't forget to thank you for helping us buy our goat. We're going to get a *great big* one!"

She scampered off happily, and even Paul almost smiled as they all watched her go. "Christmas," explained Derrick to the deputy, "is all about the children."

Purline waited until the child was out of sight to address the deputy again. "Well, if you ask me, my money is still on the Hell's Angel," she said determinedly. "Just because it's not the same man that was in the paper doesn't mean he didn't do it, and I'm telling you there's something awful suspicious about that Mick fellow."

"Again," insisted the deputy, "if I could get a complete description of the missing items, and then I'll need to interview all the guests . . ."

There was a commotion in the corridor, raised voices and slamming doors and a woman's voice demanding, "Carl! Carl, where are you?"

Leona Bartlett strode into the office, her hair wind-tossed, her color high and her gaze fierce. She was trailed by the Mathesons and the Canons, all of them still holding champagne glasses, their expressions alert and interested.

"Officer," declared Leona forcefully. "I'm an attorney and this man is my client." She swiveled a sharp gaze toward her astonished husband. "Honey, don't say another word." And then she swung back to the deputy. "This is a federal case and you have no jurisdiction here. Furthermore, my client has already signed an agreement with the state attorney general that protects him from prosecution by local authorities, so if it isn't too much trouble would you *please* tell me what's going on here?"

Paul lurched to his feet. "Federal case?"

Derrick said weakly, "Oh, this will definitely be in the paper."

Bob Matheson looked at Carl Bartlett with a quirk of admiration. "Attorney general? I never would have guessed it, old man."

"Quiet sort," agreed his friend Will. "Doesn't look like the kind to get into that much trouble."

Sheila looked at her sister with a raised eyebrow. "And we thought we had interesting lives."

Adele replied, "Of course, there is such a thing as too interesting." She sipped from her glass.

Carl just stared at his wife with a look of quiet resignation. "How did you know?"

She dug into her purse and took out a manila envelope, shaking it at him forcefully. "I found this in your nightstand—copies of your deposition and the lab reports your company falsified. The bigger question is why didn't you tell me?"

An uncertain bewilderment clouded Carl's gaze as he stared at the envelope. "But that's impossible. I left that envelope at home. I deliberately hid it where you wouldn't find it."

"Why?" she demanded, and now the ferocity in her eyes was wiped away by the sheen of tears. "Why didn't you trust me?"

Then, dashing away her tears and her own question with a single swipe of her hand, she turned back to the deputy. "Now," she demanded sternly, extending her hand, "may I see your warrant?"

The deputy began, "Ma'am, I'm here on a burglary complaint . . ."

"Burglary!" exclaimed Sheila, big eyed.

Paul smothered another groan. "We wanted to keep this quiet . . ."

Carl said to his wife, "Your Christmas gifts. The girls' watches, your necklace . . ."

"Oh, for heaven's sake!" She tossed him an impatient, disbelieving look. "Didn't you get my text? I took them with me to Richmond to return for a full refund. Do you honestly think we can afford twenty thousand dollars worth of jewelry when you don't have a job and we're facing at least that much in attorney's fees?"

The deputy closed his notebook and Paul sank again into his chair, hand over his heart. "Oh, thank goodness." Then, to the others who were crowding into the office doorway, "No cause for alarm, folks, everything is fine here. His *wife* took the jewelry."

Purline objected, "Everything is not fine! What about all that other stuff? Your train and the silver and . . ."

"My letter opener," supplied Derrick.

The deputy opened his notebook again.

"Well, of course," Paul asserted, "but at least none of that belongs to a guest. Our valuables are insured, but the trust of our guests . . . that's priceless! So I say again, thank goodness."

Derrick nodded his wholehearted agreement.

Carl took a step toward his wife. "You went to Richmond?"

"Of course I did. Blake Archer is the best attorney in the southeast, and I had to make sure to get him on our team. If we hadn't gotten the documents to the courthouse before closing today, we wouldn't have even been able to *begin* working on discovery until after the new year, and his office was the only one with the manpower to get it done."

"Wait a minute!" exclaimed Will. "You work for Apricot Foods. They had that massive recall over the summer—this has got to be some kind of whistle-blower case!"

Sheila said, "Good for you!" And lifted her glass.

Adele looked at Will suspiciously. "How did you figure that out? You didn't used to be that smart."

The deputy said, "Do you think we could get back to the case at hand?" He moved his gaze around the room, which had grown more than a little crowded. "And could everyone who does *not* have a stolen item to report please wait somewhere else? Don't leave the house though, because I'll want to talk to you all."

Adele shrugged and drained the last bubbles from her glass. "Suits me. I could use a refill."

Sheila worried, "Maybe we should do an inventory of our rooms."

Carl touched his wife's arm and they left the room, walking close together. Will, oblivious, dropped a companionable hand on Carl's shoulder and said, "So tell me about this case of yours. Is it anything like the one in upstate New York a few years back? Boy, that poor guy got the shaft."

When everyone except Purline, Paul and Derrick had left the room, the long-suffering deputy turned back to Paul. "Sir, next to the jewelry, you said the most valuable item missing was an antique train. Could you describe it, please?"

"Well," began Paul, "it was wooden. And red. Hand-carved in Holland. About so big . . ." He held out his hands a foot or so apart.

"Did it look anything like this?"

They all turned at the sound of Mrs. Hildebrand's voice. She stood at the office door with an amused look on her face, resting both hands on the crown of her walking stick. Beside her were Purline's three children, dressed in their outdoor gear and ready to go home. Naomi, the oldest, held a medium-sized plastic box in her hands, the contents of which were clearly visible to anyone who cared to look.

"The young ones here were just showing me their treasures," explained Mrs. Hildebrand.

Derrick hurried forward. "Apologies, Mrs. Hildebrand," he said. "Children, what have we been told about bothering the guests?" He stopped short as he reached them, staring at the box.

He swiveled his head toward Paul and then, in astonishment, back to the box again. "It's your train," he said. He took out the aged wooden engine and showed it to Paul, who got slowly to his feet, staring. Derrick reached into the box again, and brought out the video game console, still in its original wrapping. "Wait. Here's my letter opener, and the candlestick . . . Oh, my God, your crepe pans!"

Paul rushed forward and dug into the box, snatching out a crepe pan with one hand and a box car with the other. "They're here!" he cried, gazing at them as though upon the Holy Grail. "It's them, they're really here!" He dug back through the box and pulled out a book. "Derrick, this is your Emily Dickenson first edition! It's your most prized possession."

Derrick's face lost a little color as he grabbed

the book and stared at it for a moment in disbelief, then pressed it close to his chest. "It was on my shelf only this morning," he said. His voice sounded strangulated.

"It's very valuable," asserted one of the twins. All eyes turned on him.

"All our treasures are valuable," added the other boy.

"We're going to take them to the bank," said Naomi.

"And trade them for money," added one of the twins.

"For a goat," said the other.

Purline's hand was at her throat. "You . . ." Her voice was hoarse and her eyes bulged as she looked at the children. "You *took* these things?"

"We didn't take them," Naomi insisted earnestly. "Mr. Paul and Mr. Derrick said they wanted to help."

"With our goat," said Joshua.

"Mr. Paul said we needed valuable stuff," said Naomi.

"And Mr. Derrick said we needed a lot more money," said Joshua.

"And God helps those who help themselves," added Jacob.

The deputy closed his notebook again, trying to keep a straight face. "Gentlemen, please ascertain that everything is there. Will you be pressing charges?"

Purline reached behind her to steady herself on the corner of the desk. "My children," she whispered. "My children are thieves. I am raising criminals. My children are going to jail."

Paul looked at Derrick. The look he returned was filled with pained determination as he slowly returned the book to the box. Reluctantly, Paul did the same with the box car, and finally, with the crepe pan.

"Don't be absurd, Purline," Paul said, though with obvious difficulty. "The children were right, we offered to help."

"You wouldn't let us give them money," Derrick went on, "so we donated these things to the cause."

"Besides," added Paul, "no point in upsetting the little tykes the night before Christmas. After all, they worked hard for the goat. They deserve something for their efforts."

He managed a strained smile as he patted Naomi on the head. "Go in good cheer, little ones. Merry Christmas."

Purline fixed them both with a long hard stare, her lips tightly compressed and her churning eyes unreadable. Then, without warning, she flung herself on Paul, hugging him so hard that he staggered, and then on Derrick. "I'll make this up to you," she whispered fiercely, "if it's the last thing I do."

Derrick patted her shoulder uncertainly. "Well,

perhaps a little less starch in the whites," he suggested.

Purline stepped back, sniffed, and smoothed both hands on the sides of her jeans. She raised her chin and said, "Well. Looks like the good Lord taught me a lesson in humility this Christmas. Maybe I won't be so quick to judge next time."

Paul replied, "A good lesson for all of us."

She turned to gather up her brood, and then looked back over her shoulder, frowning a little. "Of course," she pointed out, "your van is still missing. And so is everybody in it."

Carl Bartlett moved to the window of the parlor and watched the Christmas lights pop on all around the garden—the white branch lights, the blue and pink spotlights, the cascading curtain lights. It was like looking at the sky upside down. Behind him the fire crackled and the Christmas tree sparkled and the chatter over the excitement of the last few minutes was lively. There was plenty to drink and more than enough to nibble on from the leftover tea tables, and no one seemed to want to leave. He did not want to draw attention to himself by being the first to do so. Besides, his girls still weren't back.

Leona came over to him. "I tried calling Kelly again," she said. "All I get is an out of service area message."

"I'm sure they'll be back any time now." He was amazed at how calm his voice sounded, how easy it was to have a normal conversation. "The deputy said there hadn't been any reports of accidents involving a van like theirs. It's Christmas Eve traffic."

She said quietly, "This has to have been going on for weeks. Why didn't you tell me what you were going through?"

He was silent for a moment, watching the lights. "I didn't think I had the right. I was about to blow up everybody's world. Yours, mine, the girls. I wasn't sure . . . I wasn't sure how any of you would react to what I had to tell you. So I thought if I could pretend everything was normal for just another couple of weeks . . . If we could have one last Christmas . . ."

Leona tilted her head, studying his profile, and understanding dawned slowly. "You didn't think we'd support you."

He drew a breath. He said, "I'm in charge of operations. I'm responsible for everything that goes out of that company. I should have figured out what was going on sooner, but I didn't. Charges could still be brought against me."

She said sharply, "You'll never serve a day in jail."

He couldn't quite meet her eyes. "After this comes out, I'll be virtually unemployable. We'll have to sell the house."

She gave a dismissive toss of her head. "I've

got a law degree. It won't kill me to put it to actual work for a change."

He said, "It's going to get ugly. The girls aren't used to hard times." He looked at her somberly. "You don't have to go through this with me. None of you do."

Leona replied mercilessly, "Our daughters are spoiled, ungrateful and self-centered." She wrapped her fingers around his arm, angling her body to look up at him. "They've gotten used to thinking of you as just the guy who brings home the paycheck. Maybe I have too, if I'm being perfectly honest. It's easy to take things for granted when life is rolling along the way you want it to. We've all gotten lazy and spoiled and complacent, and maybe it takes something like this to wake us up, because that all changes today. Being a family takes *work,* Carl, it's not something that just happens. And how dare you think we wouldn't stand by you." She pressed her cheek fiercely against his arm. "How dare you."

He drew her into his arms and closed his eyes, just holding her. "I love you," he said huskily. "And I'm sorry."

"Me to," she whispered. "On both counts."

She stepped away from him as headlights flashed on the window and exhaled her relief. "Thank goodness," she said. Over her shoulder she called, "Everyone! They're back!"

Derrick hurried into the kitchen, where Paul was setting up the fondue pots for the informal fireside Christmas Eve supper. "As long as the booze holds up, I think we're going to be okay," he said, rubbing his hands together anxiously. "Everyone seems to have forgotten about the burglary and moved on to gossiping about Mr. Bartlett—which, fortunately, he doesn't seem to mind. Good heavens, how many criminals can this house hold, anyway?"

"Well, thank God the only ones we're responsible for are of the juvenile variety," Paul said. "Good decision to wait until tomorrow to give Purline her gift, by the way. One more gesture of kindness tonight would have done her in, I'm afraid."

Derrick said, "You know what this makes us, don't you?"

Paul refused to answer, and Derrick supplied, "Nice."

"Well," Paul admitted grudgingly, "I suppose there are worse things to be." He handed a tray filled with fondue pots and sterno cups to Derrick. "By the way, did Mr. Phipps ever return? He left hours ago, and if he and his wife aren't going to join us for supper . . ."

Headlights flashed on the window and Derrick said, "That might be him now."

Paul turned, and then practically sagged with

relief as he recognized the profile of the vehicle. "No. Thank God, it's the van."

Derrick put down the tray with a clatter and the two of them ran out into the cold without their coats to greet the wayward travelers.

"Thank goodness!" Derrick exclaimed as the first passenger door slid open and the two teenagers climbed out, their hands filled with plastic shopping bags. "We were so worried!"

"Mildly concerned," corrected Paul, ushering the two girls up the steps, "only mildly concerned. We knew you were safe in the very competent hands of our highly insured driver."

Angela Phipps climbed out next, and her hands were also filled with bags. Moreover, she was laughing. Neither Paul nor Derrick could remember seeing her laugh since she'd been here. She was followed by Geoffery Windsor, who had apparently made the remark that made her laugh, because he was smiling too. His hands were also filled with shopping bags.

"Mr. Windsor!" exclaimed Paul, gripping his hand, "welcome back! We're so glad you changed your mind."

"Actually . . ." Geoffery began.

"We missed our flights," said Cici, who was the next to emerge.

"All of us," added Lindsay.

"The van broke down," Bridget explained.

Dismay swept both men's faces as they stared

at their rumpled, disheveled friends. They were also carrying plastic shopping bags.

"Oh, no!" Derrick exclaimed. "Oh girls, how horrible!"

"We're so sorry!" Paul added, distraught. "I don't know how this could have happened! The van is only six months old! How could this have happened?"

"Actually," Bridget said cheerfully, "it was quite an adventure. And you know what they say— everything happens for a reason."

"We just feel bad that you went to so much trouble for nothing," Cici said.

"And I hope those tickets are refundable," added Lindsay.

"We asked your driver to stop here first," Cici said, "because we knew the girls' parents would be worried."

"And I could use a bathroom," Lindsay put in.

"And we wanted to deliver these," Bridget said, holding up her two hands filled with packages.

"Well, you're staying for supper, no arguments or questions," said Derrick. He spread his arms and ushered them through the door like a hen herding chicks. "And Christmas dinner tomorrow without question. I'm just devastated your flights fell through!"

"We'll call the airlines," Paul promised, following close, "and get you on the very next availables. Don't you worry, you will be with your loved ones this holiday season, I promise you that!"

"Really," said Lindsay, "a bathroom would be just fine."

They arrived in the parlor just as the girls were piling their shopping bags at an astonished Mrs. Hildebrand's feet. "We thought it would be cool to get some stuff for those kids in Haiti," explained Pamela. She punctuated her words with a lift of her shoulders that was designed to indicate complete detachment. "You know, some toys or video games or something, stuff they can't get over there. Since it was Christmas and all."

"But then all the stores were closed," explained Kelly. "The good ones, anyway. So we ended up going to Walmart."

Pamela's parents stood a little way off, their hands entwined, staring at their daughters as though they had never seen them before.

"It was Mrs. Phipps's idea," Pamela said. "She said kids that don't have their own room need a place to keep their stuff."

"So we got backpacks," said Kelly.

"And things to put in them," Pamela said. "Books, mostly, because, well . . ." She glanced at the older woman, looking suddenly shy. "We figured they liked stories."

"But other things, too," Kelly said, upending one of the bags. "Fingernail polish and hairspray for the girls . . ."

"Tee shirts and model airplanes for the boys," said Geoffery, adding his bags to the pile.

"Sketchbooks and colored pencils," said Lindsay, placing her purchases among the others, "and crayons and coloring books for the younger ones."

"And what's Christmas without candy?" said Bridget, adding her bags. "Along with a few more practical things, like glittery toothbrushes and fun-flavored toothpaste."

"We really did have the best time," said Cici, placing her bags among the others.

Angela was the last to add her bags. "It's been so long since I went shopping on Christmas Eve," she said, "I'd forgotten how much I loved it. And shopping for children . . . well, I may have discovered a new tradition."

Behind her a voice said, "It sounds like something I'd enjoy sharing."

Angela turned to see her husband standing at the door, still wearing his coat, the wool scarf loose around his neck. She straightened up slowly and walked to him.

"I got some glitter markers," Kelly was saying, "I thought we could write each kid's name on her backpack. But you'll have to tell us what they are."

"Girls," said Mrs. Hildebrand. "I really . . . just don't know what to say."

There were tears of pride in Leona Bartlett's

eyes as Angela passed her, and she heard Carl murmur to his wife, "I think our girls are going to be okay after all."

Angela stood before Bryce, who still smelled of the cold night and leather car seats. He said, "By the time I got your note the van had already left. I went to every airport and train station. I tried to call every ten minutes." He dropped his gaze briefly. "I didn't want . . . don't want to spend the rest of my life remembering Christmas as the time I lost you, too."

He looked at her, and then, gently, reached out and took both of her hands in his large cold ones. "I shouldn't have said what I said the other night. I love you, Angela, and it doesn't even matter whether you love me back. I'm not ready to give up on us yet. I thought I was. But I'm not."

She said, "I'm glad. Because I'm not ready to give up either." Her grip tightened hesitantly, and then with more boldness, on his. She searched his eyes. "I want to talk, Bryce. I want to talk to you about what happened. I want to talk about David, about our marriage, about everything. I realized this afternoon that in all these years, after everything we've been through, we've talked to a lot of people—counselors, therapists, pastors, family, friends—but we've never really talked to each other. Can we do that now? Would that be okay?"

Everything in his face softened: his eyes, his

smile. He lifted a hand and caressed his wife's neck gently. "Yes," he said. "I think that would be okay."

Paul and Derrick hovered at the edge of the room, anxiously looking over the goings-on. "Everything seems to have worked out okay," Derrick said. "Everyone's home safe and sound, no one was arrested . . ."

"No one's suing us," Paul was quick to point out.

"All's well that ends well," said Derrick.

"I'm just broken-hearted about the girls," Paul said. "What kind of Christmas is this for them? They spent the entire day on the side of the road, their loved ones are thousands of miles away . . ."

"They're being good sports about it," Derrick said, "but I can't imagine how disappointed they must be. I almost think it would be better if we'd never gotten their hopes up." He caught his breath sharply and his eyes lit up with a sudden idea. "Do you know what we should do? We should set up a video chat with everyone! A Christmas in cyberspace!"

Paul drew a breath for a reply when his phone rang. He held up a finger for patience as he took out his phone, but Derrick ignored him.

"Cici, Bridget!" he called excitedly. "We have a simply marvelous idea! Where's Lindsay?"

Paul answered his telephone to Lori's irate

voice. "Uncle Paul!" she demanded. "Where is everyone?"

Paul had to plug one ear with his finger to block out the chatter and the laughter, certain he had misheard. "What? Lori?"

"We've been traveling for *hours!*" she exclaimed. "And then we get here and the house is all dark, and even Ida Mae's not here!"

"She's at church," Paul replied absently. Then, more alertly, "What? *What* did you say? Where are you?"

"Home!" she replied impatiently. "And believe me, it wasn't easy, either. But after Noah called we felt so bad that everyone was going to be alone on Christmas, and to tell you the truth we were getting a little tired of Cabo—it's *so* hot!—and it is our first Christmas together as a real family, so I called Dominic, because it's his first Christmas as a married person too, and it turns out his daughter had been begging him to go home and spend Christmas with Lindsay, and guess what?" She paused, more for breath than for effect. "Her company has a corporate jet! And her boss let her use it! Well, not her exactly, because she does still have a broken leg, but us! So here we all are, but where are *they?* And, oh," she added, again sucking in a breath, "there was a message on the answering machine from Carol in Chicago for Aunt Bridget, saying that the doctor had cleared her little girl to fly so they'll be coming in the day after tomorrow. So I really, really hope they all haven't taken a notion to go on a cruise or something. Because we've been traveling for *hours!*"

A slow delighted smile spread over Paul's face and he murmured, "Well, well. Sometimes things really do work out for the best."

"What?"

He said, "Light the fire and plug in the Christmas tree, darling. Your loved ones will be home momentarily."

He disconnected and tucked his phone back into his pocket, then raised his hand for attention just as Lindsay came out of the bathroom. "Oh, ladies!" he called. "Do I have a Christmas surprise for you!"

December 25

Merry Christmas, Everyone!
May the joy of the season be
in your hearts today and forever.
Your hosts,
Paul and Derrick

6:00– 10:00 a.m.	Coffee, stollen, fruit cake and Christmas wreath cinnamon rolls available in the dining room
8:30 a.m.	Christmas breakfast buffet in the dining room
10:00 a.m.	Join us for eggnog and cookies by the Christmas tree in the parlor
1:00 p.m.	Buffet luncheon in the dining room
3:00 p.m.	Christmas concert by the Killian Hills Boys Choir
5:00 p.m.	Gala Christmas cocktails served in the front parlor
7:00 p.m.	Candlelight Christmas dinner in the dining room

EIGHTEEN

Angels We Have Heard on High

T he candles were lit, the fire crackled in the parlor, and miniature white lights twinkled on every Christmas tree. A large bowl of Paul's famous eggnog was the centerpiece of the parlor buffet, surrounded by platters of colorfully decorated Christmas cookies and—a last minute addition that had arrived at seven o'clock that morning—one of Ida Mae's Christmas Angel Cakes. The old inn was awash in the fragrance of evergreen and cinnamon and the sounds of muted Christmas carols.

The guests had all gathered around the parlor Christmas tree after the breakfast buffet, some still in their slippers, to open the gifts they had brought from home and admire the treasures of others. Pamela Bartlett cried out loud in delight when she opened a surprise gift from Mrs. Hildebrand and found a new iPhone inside. Then, with her expression sobering, she said, "But if it's okay with you, I think I'll trade it in for a cheaper model." She glanced at her father who returned an encouraging smile. "We could kind of use the money."

"A wise decision, my dear," agreed Mrs.

Hildebrand, looking with approval at the girl's parents. "Very wise indeed."

Geoffery Windsor brought the older woman a cup of eggnog. "You again," she said with a downturn of her lips. But she accepted the cup in good grace. "I suppose you're here for an interview."

He raised an eyebrow. "As a matter of fact, I am."

She took a sip of the eggnog, held the cup out for an appreciative look, and sipped again. "What's this new book of yours about?"

"Everyday heroes," he replied.

She sniffed. "There are plenty of people you should be interviewing before me, then. Some of them right here in this room."

"I agree," said Geoffery. His glance fell upon Bryce and Angela Phipps whose voices he had heard murmuring behind closed doors far into the night, and moved to Carl Bartlett, who would be called many things—including hero—by many people over the next few months. Even his daughters, who had tried for one brief moment to reach beyond themselves into the lives of others, had a story to tell. He said, "And I'm going to talk to all of them. But," he added, and his eyes twinkled as he glanced down at her, "given your age, I thought it would be smart to start with you."

She chuckled. "There may be hope for you yet." She sipped her eggnog, watching him shrewdly. "Let me ask you something. What would you say if I told you there was an angel with us the whole time in that building in Haiti?"

He regarded her thoughtfully for a moment, then took a sip from his cup. "Do you know something? I just might believe you."

"Is that right?" Her eyes narrowed a fraction, sizing him up. "And what would you say if I told you I saw that same angel right here at the Hummingbird House? Talked to him, too, more than once."

Geoffery nodded slowly and replied, "Then I'd say we just might have something in common."

The faint hint of a smile curved one corner of her lips. "Well then." She finished off her eggnog and handed the empty cup to him. "Bring me another one of these, and we'll talk."

Paul pushed aside the silver wrapping paper and undid the flap of the box Derrick had given to him. A slow and quiet smile spread over his face when he saw the antique wooden train nestled inside.

"I explained to the children that they needed a licensed broker to ensure they received full price for a treasure as valuable as this," Derrick said. He frowned a little as he lifted his glass to his lips. "The little hooligans robbed me blind."

Paul put the box aside and reached under the Christmas tree for another package. "I just offered them ten dollars," he said, and presented it to Derrick.

Derrick unwrapped the package and released a long breath of relief as he pressed the copy of Emily Dickenson's *Poems* to his breast. "Thank you, Jesus," he said. And then to Paul, quickly, "And you of course, my dear." He beamed. "Thank you!"

Carefully, Derrick put the book aside and added, "Purline said she had a long talk with the children about how important it is to ask permission before helping oneself, even when the Lord is on one's side. She wanted to return everything this morning, but I told her we were sincere about our wish to donate."

Paul looked at him sharply, "Even my crepe pans?"

"Well," Derrick pointed out blandly, "a gift isn't really a gift without sacrifice, is it? And it's for the children."

Paul scowled into his drink. "That village is going to be swarming with goats."

"It's like Purline always says," replied Derrick contentedly, "where your treasure is, there will your heart be also."

Paul grumbled, "I don't even know what that means."

The subject of discussion had been sailing through the house for the past half hour, snapping sheets and fluffing pillows, grinning and humming

Christmas carols under her breath and losing absolutely no opportunity to fling her bracelet-adorned arm into the air so that the gemstones caught the light. Apparently, even Purline was not immune to the old-fashioned pleasures of a jewelry-based Christmas.

Derrick slipped his arm through Paul's. "It means," he said, "that I treasure you."

Paul slanted him a dry look that, despite his best intentions, turned to tenderness. "And I, you," he said.

They raised their glasses in a moment of smiling, mutual toast. Then Paul's brows drew together in mild concern. "I'm sorry Mick left last night before we had a chance to give him his gift card."

"Or his paycheck," added Derrick, with an even deeper frown. "Surely he'll be back for it."

"I certainly hope so."

"On the other hand," mused Derrick, "he was rather a lone ranger type, wasn't he? A little odd, altogether. Pleasant, though," he was quick to add.

"Very pleasant," agreed Paul. "And a huge help to us. He should have at least allowed us to write a reference."

"It would have been glowing."

"Absolutely vivid," Paul asserted.

"Pawsladder! Dekarrenson!"

The two men turned to see Park Sung standing

at the door, grinning broadly and waving them over with big, sweeping gestures. Paul and Derrick exchanged a puzzled look, then left their glasses on the mantle and followed as Park Sung, still grinning excitedly, led the way out of the room to the spa.

Earlier that morning Derrick had tried to explain the festively wrapped gift card he had presented to them, receiving only polite but baffled looks until he finally retrieved the gift card, exchanged it for cash, and said simply, "Tip." That was apparently a word they understood because both faces cleared as they began to smile and bow their gratitude. Feeling rather festive himself, Derrick had booked a massage for both himself and Paul later that afternoon; he hoped they hadn't misunderstood the time.

Kim Gi, dressed in her white working kimono and black slacks—feet bare, of course—stood outside the spa door. Her hands were tucked formally into her kimono sleeves, but she was grinning with as much excitement as was Park Sung, who practically skipped the last few steps. Kim Gi bowed when she saw them, and opened the door to the spa.

"Oh dear," murmured Derrick, glancing at his watch, "I'm afraid they did misunderstand the time. I scheduled for three."

But before he could even begin to try to explain the error, Park Sung began gesticulating wildly, hopping up and down as he beckoned them inside with sweeping arm gestures. "Hahmonee!" he declared. "Hahmonee!"

Paul looked at Derrick and repeated, "Harmony?"

Derrick shrugged, as confused as Paul was. They saw no choice other than to follow Park Sung inside.

He led the way to the massage room and opened it with a flourish. "Soo. Prize," he announced. Hesitantly the two men looked around.

The room was a peaceful oasis of variegated shades of green, calm winter light filtering through the transparent window shade. Flickering candles smelled of lemongrass and balsam, and the soothing sounds of a lute played a melody against the background sounds of a waterfall. All was exactly as it had been designed, except when Derrick moved his eyes toward the ceiling. He clutched Paul's arm, speechless, and Paul tilted his head to look upwards as well.

The entire ceiling was covered with a mural magnificent enough to rival any fresco in any palazzo in Italy. Cerulean blue skies and gold-tipped clouds provided a heavenly backdrop for the angels, dozen of them. There were blond angels, brunette angels, male angels, female angels, young angels, old angels. There was one angel with long blonde curls that looked suspiciously like Harmony. And another . . .

"Oh, my God," Derrick whispered. "It's you!"

Paul nodded slowly and turned his head meaningfully in another direction. Derrick followed his gaze. "And me," he added.

"It's actually rather . . . mesmerizing," Paul admitted after a moment.

"Like a train wreck in heaven," agreed Derrick, his head still tilted back. "You want to look away, but you can't."

Park Sung stood close by, his head also tilted to the ceiling, beaming proudly. "Hahmonee," he said.

Paul and Derrick tore their eyes away from the ceiling and met each other's gaze with a smile. "Surprise," they said in unison.

Bryce Phipps stood with one hand on the back of his wife's chair, watching her face as she accepted the blue-foil wrapped box he offered to her. Around them the others laughed and chatted, Christmas carols played, glass hummingbirds caught the lights on the Christmas tree and seemed to flutter their wings in delight. Their hosts returned to the room with another pitcher of eggnog and an armload of firewood. Yet the two of them, though in the middle of the gaiety and activity, had surrounded themselves with a gentle veil of privacy through which others could look, but not intrude.

"I know you said no gifts," Bryce said quietly. "But I've waited for years to give you this. When we came here, I thought it would be my last chance. Now I just think it's time."

She looked at him uncertainly. "What is it?"

"I have no idea," he admitted. "David got it for you that Christmas . . . the Christmas before he died. He had the store wrap it for him and he wouldn't tell me what it was." He smiled a little, remembering. "Although he was dropping so many hints I'm sure he would have blurted it out in another day or two."

Angela dropped her eyes to the package in her lap, her hand hesitant, making no move to unwrap it. She said softly, "He'll always be with us, won't he?"

Her husband slipped his hand beneath her hair, caressing her neck. "I hope so. And I think it's up to us to make sure he is."

Angela slit the tape with her fingernail and folded back the paper. She opened the box and removed the soft packing material. For a moment she just stared, in wonder and disbelief, at what was inside.

"Oh my goodness," she whispered. "I remember this."

Slowly, she drew the snow globe out of the box and held it up to the light. She turned it upside down and then right-side up, watching the snow swirl around the wooden house with the different colored painted doors. She couldn't help herself. Holding her breath, she peered more closely, looking into the golden windows. But as hard as she tried, she couldn't see inside. And then she realized it didn't matter. Because she was already here.

She laughed out loud in delight. "Look!" she exclaimed. "It's just like this place!"

Everyone crowded around to see, and even Paul and Derrick were impressed by the resemblance. "What do you know about that, old man?" Paul declared. "Our fame is even more widespread than we knew!"

"We must try to find one like it," agreed Derrick. "It would look divine on the reception desk. Do you mind my asking where you got it?"

Angela just shared a smile with her husband and replied, "I'm afraid they don't make these anymore."

What had the man in the store said when she'd asked what would happen to the people inside the globe? *They'll go on living their lives.* That was it. She reached up and clasped her husband's hand, pressing it against her shoulder, smiling. "Thank you," she said.

They'll go on living their lives.

"Hey," Kelly Bartlett said. She crawled under the Christmas tree and brought out another package, this one wrapped in silver. "There's another present here." She looked at the tag. "It's for you guys," she said, handing the package to Derrick. "Both of you."

They exchanged one of those delighted Christmas morning who-can-this-be-from looks, and Derrick tore off the wrapping.

"You are such a heathen," Paul complained affectionately, trying to salvage the wrapping paper Derrick had discarded. "Reclaim, reuse, recycle."

"Will you look at this?" Derrick held up a polished wooden plaque for everyone to admire. "Isn't this lovely?"

"Beautiful craftsmanship," agreed Paul. "What's engraved on it?"

"It says . . ." Derrick turned the plaque around and read out loud, "Don't be afraid to show kindness to strangers, for thereby many have entertained angels unaware."

"Well," Paul said, a little uncertainly, "what a lovely sentiment."

"Perfect for our front hallway," Derrick suggested.

"Is there a card?"

Derrick dug back into the box and came up with a folded sheet of paper. "Ah," he said, smiling. "It says 'Thanks for the hospitality, Mick.' "

"Well now." Paul's smile broadened as he took the plaque and admired it. "Isn't that nice? I always did say he was a man of class and distinction."

"Multilayered," agreed Derrick.

Paul's expression was considering. "A little odd," he admitted.

"But nice," Derrick said.

Across the room, Geoffery Windsor looked at Mrs. Hildebrand and winked. She smiled back, and both of them lifted their cups in the air in a silent toast.

December 26

Thank you for making the Hummingbird House your holiday destination! Check-out is at 11:00 a.m. Airport transportation will be waiting at the main entrance. Please enjoy a farewell champagne brunch with us in the dining room beginning at 9:00 a.m. We hope your stay has been as memorable for you as it has been for us and that you will allow us the pleasure of your company as soon as your schedule permits. In the meantime we will hold you in our hearts until we meet again. Safe travels and Happy New Year—

Your hosts,
Paul and Derrick

ABOUT THE AUTHOR

Donna Ball is the author of over a hundred novels under several different pseudonyms in a variety of genres that include romance, mystery, suspense, paranormal, western adventure, historical and women's fiction. Recent popular series include the Ladybug Farm series, The Hummingbird House series, The Dogleg Island Mystery series, and the Raine Stockton Dog Mystery series. Donna is an avid dog lover and her dogs have won numerous titles for agility, obedience and canine musical freestyle. She lives in a restored Victorian Barn in the heart of the Blue Ridge mountains with a variety of four-footed companions. You can contact her at http://www.donnaball.net.

Center Point Large Print
600 Brooks Road / PO Box 1
Thorndike, ME 04986-0001 USA

(207) 568-3717

US & Canada:
1 800 929-9108
www.centerpointlargeprint.com